SHERSTON'S PROGRESS

Also by Siegfried Sassoon

THE COMPLETE MEMOIRS OF GEORGE SHERSTON
hard covers and in Faber Paperbacks

MEMOIRS OF A FOX-HUNTING MAN
Faber Paperbacks

MEMOIRS OF AN INFANTRY OFFICER
Faber Paperbacks

SELECTED POEMS
Faber Paperbacks

SIEGFRIED'S JOURNEY 1916–20
Faber Paperbacks

Edited by Rupert Hart-Davis

WAR POEMS OF SIEGFRIED SASSOON
hard covers and in Faber Paperbacks

SIEGFRIED SASSOON DIARIES 1915–18
hard covers

SIEGFRIED SASSOON DIARIES 1920–22
hard covers

SHERSTON'S PROGRESS

by

SIEGFRIED SASSOON

faber and faber

*First published in 1936
by Faber and Faber Limited
3 Queen Square London WC1N 3AU
First published in Faber Paperbacks in 1983
Printed in Great Britain by
Whitstable Litho Ltd Whitstable Kent
All rights reserved*

British Library Cataloguing in Publication Data

Sassoon, Siegfried
Sherston's progress.
I. Title
823'.912[F]   PR6037.A86
ISBN 0-571-13033-X

CONTENTS

" I told him that I was a Pilgrim going to the Celestial City."

PART ONE: RIVERS

I

To be arriving at a shell-shock hospital in a state of un-militant defiance of military authority was an experience peculiar enough to stimulate my speculations about the immediate future. In the train from Liverpool to Edin-burgh I speculated continuously. The self-dramatizing ele-ment in my mind anticipated something sensational. After all, a mad-house would be only a few degrees less grim than a prison, and I was still inclined to regard myself in the role of a "ripe man of martyrdom". But the unhistrionic part of my mind remembered that the neurologist member of my medical board had mentioned someone called Rivers. "Rivers will look after you when you get there." I inferred, from the way he said it, that to be looked after by Rivers was a stroke of luck for me. Rivers was evidently some sort of great man; anyhow his name had obvious free associ-ations with pleasant landscapes and unruffled estuaries.

Slateford War Hospital was about twenty minutes in a taxi from Edinburgh. In peace-time it had been a "hydro", and it was a gloomy cavernous place even on a fine July afternoon. But before I'd been inside it five minutes I was actually talking to Rivers, who was dressed as an R.A.M.C. captain. There was never any doubt about my liking him. He made me feel safe at once, and seemed to know all about me. What he didn't know he soon found out.

Readers of my previous volumes will be aware that I am no exception to the rule that most people enjoy talking about themselves to a sympathetic listener. Next morning I went to Rivers' room as one of his patients. In an hour's talk I told him as much as I could about my perplexities. Forgetting that he was a doctor and that I was an "inter-esting case", I answered his quiet impartial questions as

clearly as I could, with a comfortable feeling that he understood me better than I understood myself.

For the first few days, we had one of these friendly confabulations every evening. I had begun by explaining that
my "attitude", as expressed in my "statement", was unchanged. "Just because they refused to court martial me,
it doesn't make any difference to my still being on strike,
does it?" I remarked. (This fact was symbolized by my
tunic, which was still minus the M.C. ribbon that I had
thrown into the River Mersey!)

Rivers replied that my safest plan would be to mark
time for a few weeks; meanwhile the hospital authorities
would allow me all the freedom I wanted and would rely
on me not to do anything imprudent. One evening I asked
whether he thought I was suffering from shell-shock.

"Certainly not," he replied.

"What *have* I got, then?"

"Well, you appear to be suffering from an anti-war
complex." We both of us laughed at that. Rivers never
seemed elderly; though there were more than twenty years
between us, he talked as if I were his mental equal, which
was very far from being the case.

Meanwhile my main problem was how to fill up my
time. Everything possible was done to make the hospital
pleasant for its inmates, but the fact remained that most of
the "other patients" weren't feeling as happy as they used
to do. The place was a live museum of war neuroses—in
other words the hospital contained about 150 officers who
had been either shattered or considerably shaken by their
war experience. I shared a room with a cheerful young
Scotch captain who showed no symptom of eccentricity,
though I gradually ascertained that he had something on
his mind—was it some hallucination about his having been
shot at by a spy?—I have forgotten, and only remember
that he was a thoroughly nice man. On the whole, I felt
happier outside the hydro than in it, so I went for long
walks on the Pentland Hills, which really did seem unaware
that there was a war on, while retaining their commemora-
tive associations with Robert Louis Stevenson. But at the

end of my first week at Slateford my career as a public
character was temporarily resuscitated by my "statement"
being read out in the House of Commons. Referring to
Hansard's *Parliamentary Debates*, 30th July, 1917, I find that
the episode occurred at 7 p.m. There, I think, it may safely
be allowed to remain at rest, unless I decide to reprint the
proceedings as an appendix to this volume, which is im-
probable. I will only divulge that the debate ended by Mr.
Bryce saying "We know that the Croats, the Serbs, the
Slovaks, the Slovenes, and the Czechs are all opposed to
it." (What they were opposed to was the Austrian dynasty,
not my statement.) Oddly enough, the name of the commandant of Slateford Hospital was also Bryce, which only
shows what a small place the world is.

As far as I was concerned the only visible result was a
batch of letters from people who either agreed or disagreed
with my views. But I needed a holiday from that sort of
thing. The intensity of my individual effort to influence the
Allied Governments had abated.

At intervals I reminded myself that my enormous gesture was still, so to speak, "on show", but I unconsciously
allowed myself to relax the mental effort required to sus-
tain it. My "attitude" was, indeed, unchanged; it had
merely ceased to be aggressive. I didn't even feel annoyed
when a celebrated novelist (for whose opinion I had asked)
wrote: "Your position cannot be argumentatively de-
fended. What is the matter with you is spiritual pride. The
overwhelming majority of your fellow-citizens are against
you." Anyhow a fellow-citizen (who was an equally famous
novelist) wrote that it was a "very striking act", and I was
grateful for the phrase. (How tantalizing of me to omit
their names! But somehow I feel that if I were to put them
on the page my neatly contrived little narrative would
come sprawling out of its frame.) Grateful I was, and not
annoyed; nevertheless it was obvious that I couldn't per-
form that sort of striking act more than once and in the
meantime I acted on the advice of Rivers and wired to
Aunt Evelyn for my golf clubs, which arrived next day,
maybe accelerated by three very fully addressed labels, all

inscribed "urgent". Simultaneously arrived a postcard from one of the overwhelming majority of my fellow-citizens who kept his name dark, but expressed his opinion that "Men like you who are willing to shake the bloody hand of the Kaiser are not worthy to call themselves Britons". This struck me as unjust; I'd never offered to shake the old Kaiser's hand, though I should probably have been considerably impressed if he'd offered to shake mine, for an emperor is an emperor all the world over even if he has done his best to wipe you off the face of the earth with high-explosive shells. As regards Aunt Evelyn, (who had a pretty poor opinion of the Kaiser) the *Morning Post* had now put her in full possession of the facts about my peace-propagating manifesto. No doubt she was delighted to know that I was well out of harm's way. The Under-Secretary of State had informed the House of Commons that I was suffering from a nervous breakdown and not responsible for my actions, which was good enough for Aunt Evelyn, and, as Rivers remarked, very much what I might have expected. Very soon I was slicing my tee-shots into the long grass on the nearest golf course. "I don't know what I'm doing," I exclaimed (referring to my swing and not to my recent political activity).

*   *   *

For me, the War felt as if it were a long way off while the summer of 1917 was coming to an end. Except for keeping an eye on the casualty lists, I did my best to turn my back on the entire business. Once, when I saw that one of my best friends had been killed, I lapsed into angry self-pity, and told myself that the War was "a sham and a stinking lie", and succeeded in feeling bitter against the unspecific crowd of non-combatants who believed that to go through with it to the end was the only way out. But on the whole I was psychologically passive—content to mark time on the golf links and do some steady reading after dinner. The fact remained that, when I awoke in the morning, my first conscious thought was no longer an unreprieved awareness that the War would go on indefinitely and that sooner or later I should be killed or mutilated. The prospect of being imprisoned as a war-resister had also evaporated. To wake up knowing that I was going to bicycle off to play two rounds of golf was not a penance. It was a reward. Three evenings a week I went along to Rivers' room to give my anti-war complex an airing. We talked a lot about European politicians and what they were saying. Most of our information was derived from a weekly periodical which contained translations from the foreign Press. What the politicians said no longer matters, as far as these memoirs of mine are concerned, though I would give a lot for a few gramophone records of my talks with Rivers. All that matters is my remembrance of the great and good man who gave me his friendship and guidance. I can visualize him, sitting at his table in the late summer twilight, with his spectacles pushed up on his forehead and his hands clasped in front of one knee; always communicating his integrity of mind; never revealing that he was weary as he must often have been after long days of exceptionally tiring work on those war neuroses which demanded such an exercise of sympathy and detachment combined. Remembering all that, and my egotistic unawareness of the possibility that I was often wasting his time and energy, I am consoled by the certainty that he did, on the whole, find me a refreshing companion. He liked me and he believed in me.

As an R.A.M.C. officer, he was bound to oppose my "pacifist tendency", but his arguments were always indirect. Sometimes he gently indicated inconsistencies in my impulsively expressed opinions, but he never contradicted me. Of course the weak point about my "protest" had been that it was evoked by personal feeling. It was an emotional idea based on my war experience and stimulated by the acquisition of points of view which I accepted uncritically. My intellect was not an ice-cold one. It was, so to speak, suffering from trench fever. I could only see the situation from the point of view of the troops I had served with; and the existence of supposedly iniquitous war aims among the Allies was for that reason well worth believing in—and inveighing against. Rivers suggested that peace at that time would constitute a victory for Pan-Germanism and nullify all the sacrifices we had made. He could see no evidence that militarism was yet discredited in Germany. On one occasion, when the pros and cons had got me well out of my depth as a debater, I exclaimed, "It doesn't seem to me to matter much what one does so long as one believes it is right!" In the silence that ensued I was aware that I had said something particularly fatuous, and hurriedly remarked that the people in Germany must be getting jolly short of food. I was really very ignorant, picking up my ideas as I went along, and rather like the man who said that he couldn't think unless he was wearing his spectacles. But Rivers always led me quietly past my blunders (though he looked a bit pained when I inadvertently revealed that I did not know the difference between "intuition" and "instinct"—which was, I suppose, one of the worst mistakes I could have made when talking to an eminent psychologist).

* * *

Among the wholesome activities of the hospital was a monthly magazine, aptly named *The Hydra*. In the September number, of which I have preserved a copy, the editorial begins as follows: "Many of us who came to the hydro slightly ill are now getting dangerously well. In this excellent concentration camp we are fast recovering from the shock of coming to England."

Outwardly, Slateford War Hospital was rather like that —elaborately cheerful. Brisk amusements were encouraged, entertainments were got up, and serious cases were seldom seen downstairs. The patients were of course unaware of the difficulties with which the medical staff had to contend. A handful of highly-qualified civilians in uniform were up against the usual red-tape ideas. War hospitals for nervous disorders were few, and the military authorities regarded them as experiments which needed careful watching and firm handling. After the War Rivers told me that the local Director of Medical Services nourished a deep-rooted prejudice against Slateford, and actually asserted that he "never had and never would recognize the existence of such a thing as shell-shock". When inspecting the hospital he "took strong exception" to the fact that officers were going about in slippers. I mention this to show how fortunate I was to have escaped contact with less enlightened army doctors, some of whom might well have aggravated me into extreme cussedness.

It was perhaps excusable that the War Office looked on Slateford with a somewhat fishy eye. The delicate problem of "lead-swingers" was involved; and in the eyes of the War Office a man was either wounded or well unless he had some officially authorized disease. Damage inflicted on the mind did not count as illness. If "war neuroses" were indiscriminately encouraged, half the expeditionary force might go sick with a touch of neurasthenia. Apparently it did not occur to the Director of Medical Services that Rivers and his colleagues were capable of diagnosing a "lead-swinger". In any case I don't think there were many of them at Slateford, and the doubtful ones were mostly men who had failed to stay the course through lack of stamina. Too much had been asked of them.

And there was I, a healthy young officer, dumped down among nurses and nervous wrecks. During my second month at the hydro I think I began to feel a sense of humiliation. (Was it "spiritual pride", I wonder, or merely the remains of *esprit de corps*?)

With my "fellow-breakdowns" I avoided war talk as far as was possible. Most of them had excellent reasons for disliking that theme; others talked about it because they couldn't get it off their minds, or else spoke of it facetiously in an effort to suppress their real feelings. Sometimes I had an uncomfortable notion that none of them respected one another; it was as though there were a tacit understanding that we were all failures, and this made me want to reassure myself that I wasn't the same as the others. "After all, I haven't broken down; I've only broken out," I thought, one evening at the end of September, as I watched the faces opposite me at the dinner table. Most of them were average types who appeared to be getting "dangerously well". But there were some who looked as if they wouldn't have had much success in life at the best of times. I was sitting between two bad stammerers—victims of "anxiety neurosis" as the saying went—(one could easily imagine "anxiety neurosis" as a staple front-line witticism). Conversation being thus impeded, I could devote my mind to wondering why I'd been playing my mashie shots so atrociously that afternoon. Up at the top table I could see Rivers sitting among the staff. He never seemed to be giving more than half his attention to what he was eating. He looked rather as though he needed a rest and I wondered how I should get on while he was away on his two weeks' leave which was due to begin next day. I supposed it would give me a chance to think out my position, which was becoming a definite problem. So far my ten weeks' respite had been mainly a pilgrimage in pursuit of a ball, and I had familiarized myself with the ups and downs of nearly all the golf courses around Edinburgh. The man I played with most days was an expert. He had been submarined on a hospital ship, but this didn't prevent him playing a good scratch game. His temper wasn't quite normal when things went wrong and he looked like losing his half-crown, but that may have been a peace-time failing also. Anyhow he was exercising a greatly improving influence on my iron shots, which had always been a weak point, and I take this opportunity of thanking him for many most enjoyable games. The way in which he laid his short approach shots stone-dead was positively fiendish.

As a purely public character I was now a complete backnumber. Letters no longer arrived from utter strangers who also wanted the War to stop. The only one I'd had lately was from someone whose dottiness couldn't be wholeheartedly denied. "My dear Boy, or Man," it began, "on August 4th, 1914, I received a message from Heaven in broad daylight, which told me that Germany must go down for ever and Russia will become rich. I have thirty relations fighting and my business is ruined." He didn't tell me what his business was. I wondered how he'd got hold of my address. . . .

The man opposite me, an habitual humorist, remarked

to the orderly who was handing him a plate of steamed pudding, "Third time this week! I shall write to the War Office and complain." I felt a sudden sense of the unreality of my surroundings. Reality was on the other side of the Channel, surely.

After dinner I went straight up to my room as usual, intending to go on with Barbusse's book which I was reading in the English translation. I will not describe the effect it was creating in my mind; I need only say that it was a deeply stimulating one. Someone was really revealing the truth about the Front Line. But that evening I failed to settle down to *Under Fire*. The room felt cheerless and uncomfortable; the unshaded light from the ceiling annoyed my eyes; very soon I found myself becoming internally exasperated with everything, myself included. It was one of those occasions when one positively enjoys hating something. So I sat there indulging in acute antagonism toward anyone whose attitude to the War was what I called "complacent"—people who just accepted it as inevitable and then proceeded to do well out of it, or who smugly performed the patriotic jobs which enabled them to congratulate themselves on being part of the National Effort.

At this point the nurse on duty whisked into the room to make sure that everything was all right and that I was keeping cheerful. She too was part of the national effort to remain bright and not give way to war neuroses. Continuing my disgruntled ruminations, I decided that I didn't dislike violent Jingos as much as acquiescent moderates, though my pacifism was strong enough to make me willing to punch the nose of anyone who disagreed with me. (Was that steamed pudding disagreeing with the boiled beef, by the way?) I thought, with ill-humoured gratitude, of the people who were contending against the cant which was current about the War, comparing their unconformity with the aggravating omniscience of the novelist whose letter had assured me that "for various reasons we civilians are better able to judge the War as a whole than you soldiers. There is no sort of callousness in this." "Business as usual" was his motto. The War had stimulated rather than dis-

couraged his output of journalism and fiction. They all
knew how to win the War—in their highly paid articles!
Damn them, I thought; and then painfully remembered
how much I had liked that particular novelist when I met
him in London. And here I was, doing my best to hate
him! (Rivers would probably say that hate was a "defin-
itely physiological condition".)

But my unprofitable meditations were now conclusively
interrupted by the arrival of my room companion—not the
cheerful young Scot in tartan breeches, but an older man
who had replaced him a few weeks before. I will call him
the Theosophist, since he was of that way of thinking (and
overdid it a bit in conversation). The Theosophist was a
tall fine-looking man with iron-grey hair and rather handsome eyes. His attitude toward me was avuncular, tolerant, and at times slightly tutorial. In peace time he had
been to some extent a man about town. He had, I assumed,
come back from the front suffering from not being quite
young enough to stand the strain, which doesn't surprise
me now that I am old enough to compare his time of life
with my own.

Anyhow he sauntered amiably in, wearing his monocle
and evidently feeling all the better for his rubber or two of
bridge. Unfortunately he "came in for" the aftermath of
my rather morose ruminations, for I was fool enough to
begin grumbling about the War and the state of society in
general.

The Theosophist responded by assuring me that we
were all only on the great stairway which conducts us to
higher planes of existence, and when I petulantly enquired
what he thought about conscripted populations slaughter-
ing one another, on the great stairway, in order to safeguard democracy and liberty, he merely replied: "Ah,
Sherston, that is the Celestial Surgeon at work upon
humanity." "Look here," I answered with unusual bril-
liance, "you say that you won a lot of prizes with your
Labradors. Did the president of Cruft's Dog Show encour-
age all the exhibits to bite one another to death?"

This irreverent repartee reduced him to a dignified

silence, after which he made a prolonged scrutiny of his
front teeth in the shaving glass. Next day, no doubt, I
made (and he accepted with old-world courtesy) what he
would have called the "amende honorable".

*   *   *

Autumn was asserting itself, and a gale got up that night.
I lay awake listening to its melancholy surgings and rum-
blings as it buffeted the big building. The longer I lay
awake the more I was reminded of the troops in the line.
There they were, stoically enduring their roofless discomfort while I was safe and warm. The storm sounded like a
vast lament and the rain was coming down in torrents. I
thought of the Ypres salient, that morass of misery and
doom. I'd never been there, but I almost wished I was
there now. It was, of course, only an emotional idea induced by the equinoctial gale; it was, however, an idea
that had its origins in significant experience. One didn't
feel like that for nothing.

It meant that the reality of the War had still got its grip
on me. Those men, so strangely isolated from ordinary
comforts in the dark desolation of murderously-disputed
trench-sectors, were more to me than all the despairing
and war-weary civilians.

Just as it was beginning to get light I awoke from an uneasy slumber. The storm had ceased and an uncertain
glimmer filtered faintly into the room through the tall
thinly-curtained window. In this semi-twilight I saw a figure standing near the door.

I stared intently, wondering who on earth it could be at
that hour, and possibly surmising that one of the patients
was walking in his sleep. The face and head were undis-
cernible, but I identified a pale buff-coloured "British
Warm" coat. Young Ormand always wore a coat like that
up in the line, and I found myself believing that Ormand
was standing by the door. But Ormand was killed six
months ago, I thought. Then the Theosophist, who was
always a bad sleeper, turned over in his bed on the other
side of the room. I was sitting up, and I could see him

looking across at me. While I waited a long minute I could hear his watch ticking on the table. The figure by the door had vanished. "Did you see anyone come into the room?" I asked. He hadn't seen anyone. Perhaps I hadn't either. But it was an odd experience.

II

While composing these apparently interminable memoirs there have been moments when my main problem was what to select from the "long littleness"—or large untidiness—of life. Although a shell-shock hospital might be described as an epitome of the after-effects of the "battle of life" in its most unmitigated form, nevertheless while writing about Slateford I suffer from a shortage of anything to say. The most memorable events must have occurred in my cranium. While Rivers was away on leave only one event occurred which now seems worth recording. The sun was shining brightly and I was giving my golf clubs a rub up after breakfast, when an orderly brought me a mysterious message. Doctor Macamble had called to see me. I had no notion who he was, but I was told that he was waiting in the entrance hall. Let me say at once that I do not know for certain whether Doctor Macamble has "passed to where beyond these voices there is peace". But, whatever his whereabouts may be at the moment of writing, in October 1917 he was, to put it plainly, a quiet-looking man who talked too much. I will go even further and suggest that at least half the time he was talking through his hat—that brown and broad-brimmed emblem of a cerebral existence —which he was holding in his left hand when I first encountered his luminous eye in the hall of the hospital.

"Second-Lieutenant Sherston?" He grasped my hand retentively.

Now to be addressed as "Second-Lieutenant" when one happens to be drawing army pay for refusing to go on being one was not altogether appropriate; and the—for him—undiffuse greeting struck me as striking an unreal

note. Had he said, "Dr. Livingstone, I presume," I should
have accepted his hand with a fuller conviction that he was
a kindred spirit. But he went from bad to worse and did it
again. "Second-Lieutenant Sherston," he continued in a
voice which more than "filled the hall"; "I am here to
offer you my profoundest sympathy and admiration for the
heroic gesture which has made your name such a . . ." (here
he hesitated, and I wondered if he was going to say "by-
word") . . . "such a bugle-call to your brother pacifists."
Here, ignoring my sister pacifists, he relinquished my hand
and became confidential. "My name is Macamble. I ven-
ture to hope that it is not altogether unknown to you. And
I have been so bold as to call on you, in the belief that I
can be of some assistance to you in the inexpressibly painful confinement to which you are being subjected." At this
juncture the man with whom I was going to play golf
paraded impatiently past us, clattering his clubs. "What
you must have endured!" he went on, moderating his
voice at last, as if he had just remembered that we might
be "overheard by an unfriendly ear". "More than two
months among men driven mad by gun-fire! I marvel that
you have retained your reason." (I might have reminded
him that he hadn't yet ascertained that I really had retained it; but I merely glanced furtively at my golfing part-
ner, whose back-view, with legs wide apart, was to be seen
on the strip of grass in front of the hydro, solemnly swinging a brassy at an imaginary ball.) Doctor Macamble now
proposed that we should take a little walk together; he
very much wanted to discuss the whole question of the
"Stop-the-War Campaign". But I very much wanted to
stop being talked to by Doctor Macamble, so I said that
I'd got to go and see my doctor. "Ah, the famous Dr.
Rivers!" he murmured, with what appeared to be a con-
spiratorial glance. He then invited me to go down to Edinburgh and continue our conversation, and I agreed to do
so on the following afternoon. I couldn't very well refuse
point-blank, and in any case I was due there for a hair-cut.

*   *   *

The aforementioned assignation was fixed for five o'clock in the lounge of the Caledonian Hotel; but I came down from Slateford by an early afternoon tramcar and spent a couple of hours strolling contentedly about the city, which happened to be looking its best in the hazy sunshine of one of those mild October days which induce mellow meditations. After my monastical existence at the hospital I found Princes Street a very pleasant promenading place. The War did not seem to have deprived Edinburgh of any of its delightful dignity; and when I thought of Liverpool, where I wandered about with my worries in July, my preference for Edinburgh was beyond question. The town-dweller goes out into the country to be refreshed by the stillness, and whatever else he may find there in the way of wild flowers, woods, fields, far-off hills, and the nobly-clouded skies which had somehow escaped his notice while he walked to and fro with his eyes on the ground. Those who live on the land come into the city and—if they are sensible people with an aptitude for experiencing—see it as it really is. It always pleases me to watch simple country people loitering about the London pavements, staring at everything around them and being bumped into by persons pressed for time who are part of that incessant procession which is loosely referred to as "the hive of human activity". All this merely indicates that although I arrived in Edinburgh with a couple of hours to spare and had nothing definite to do except to have a hair-cut, nevertheless I found no difficulty in filling up the time by gazing at shop-windows, faces, and architectural vistas, while feeling that I was very lucky to be alive on that serenely sunlit afternoon.

Waiting for Doctor Macamble in the lounge of the Caledonian Hotel wasn't quite such good value. Life was there, of course, offering itself ungrudgingly as material to be observed and ultimately transmuted into memoirs; but it was lounge life, and the collop of it which I indiscriminately absorbed was—well, I will record it without labouring the metaphor any further. (The word collop, by the way, is inserted for the sake of its Caledonian associations.) I sat myself down within easy hearing distance of a well-dressed yellow-haired woman with white eyelashes; she was having tea with an unemphatic-looking major with a sandy moustache. The subjects undergoing discussion were Socialism, Pacifism, Ramsay MacDonald, and Snowden, and the major was acting as audience. His fair companion was "fairly on her hind-legs" about it all. Pacifists, she complained, were worse than the Germans. As for MacDonald and Snowden—"I only hope that if they do start their beloved revolution," she exclaimed, "they'll both be strung up to the nearest lamp-post by the soldiers they are now trying to betray."

"Well, Mabel, I suppose you're old enough to know your own mind," replied the stalwart and sleepy-eyed major.

"And what will *you* do, Archie, if there's ever a revolution?" she enquired.

"Oh, hide, I suppose," he answered.

"Really, Archie, I sometimes wonder how you came to be my cousin!" She handed him back his automatic cigarette-lighter, which he closed with a click, looking as if he'd prefer to be competing for the scratch medal at Prestwick or Muirfield instead of hearing pacifists consigned to perdition. The hotel musicians then struck up with Mendelssohn's (German) Spring Song, to which she was supplying a self-possessed and insouciant tra-la-la when Doctor Macamble trotted in with profuse apologies for being late.

The outspoken utterances of Mabel had at all events made me feel decidedly "pro-Macamble", but I took the wise precaution of moving him a few tables further away from her. I assumed that after hearing even a modicum of his anti-war eloquence she would be more than likely to join in, and might conceivably order her cousin Archie to frog-march the doctor out of the lounge; in fact, I feared that she might regard it as her duty to break up our little pacifist meeting, thinly attended though it was.

Before rendering my account of the meeting I must explain that Macamble was a doctor not of medicine but of philosophy—a Ph.D. in fact—which may have been the

cause of his being so chock-full of ideas and adumbrations.
Urbanely regarding him across an interval of eighteen
years I find him quite unobnoxious; but I must candidly
confess that I obtained no edification while bearing the
brunt of his fussy and somewhat muddled enthusiasm.
After listening to him for about an hour and a half I could
be certain of one thing only—that he believed himself to be
rather a great man. And like so many of us who maintain
that belief, he had so far found very few people to agree
with him in his optimistic self-estimate. I suspect that he
looked on me as a potential disciple; anyhow he urgently
desired to shepherd me along the path to a salvation which
was, unquestionably, the exact antithesis to army life.
Transmogrified into a music-hall ditty, Macamble's attitude to army officers would have worked out something
like this:

> *I couldn't shake hands with a Colonel*
> *And Majors I muchly detest:*
> *All Captains to regions infernal*
> *I consign with both gusto and zest:*
> *To Subalterns blankly uncivil,*
> *I pronounce as my final belief*
> *That the man most akin to the "divvle"*
> *Is that fiend—the Commander-in-Chief.*

I could manage to be amused by that sort of artless intolerance; but when "about the second hour" he became
disposed to speak disparagingly of Rivers, I realized that
he was exceeding the limit. How much he knew about
Rivers I didn't enquire. What he did was to imply that a
subtly disintegrating influence was at work on my pacifist
zealotry, and after these preliminaries he disclosed the plan
which he had formulated for my liberation from the machi-
nations of that uniformed pathologist. With all the good-
will in the world, Doctor Macamble advised me to ab-
scond from Slateford. I had only to take a train to London,
and once I was there he would arrange for me to be exam-
ined by an "eminent alienist" who would infallibly certify
that I was completely normal and entirely responsible for

my actions. The word "alienist" was one of many whose exact meaning I had never identified in the dictionary. (I dimly associated it with a celebrated Italian named Lombroso who probably wasn't an alienist at all.) Macamble's man, he explained, was well known through his articles in the Press; but unfortunately it transpired that it was the popular rather than the pathological Press—the *Daily Mail*, in fact. I suppose I ought to have waxed indignant, but all I thought was, "Good Lord, he's trying to persuade me to do the dirty on Rivers!" Keeping this thought to myself, I remained reticent and parted from him with the heartiest of handshakes. Did I ever see him again, I wonder? And have I been too hard on him? Well, I can only say that nothing I can do to Doctor Macamble could be worse than his advice to me—had I been imbecile enough to act on it.

*　　　　*　　　　*

On a pouring wet afternoon a day or two later I was in the entrance hall of the hospital, indulging in some horseplay with another young officer who happened to be feeling "dangerously well" at the moment. It was the hour when visitors came to see patients, and my somewhat athletic sense of humour had focused itself on a very smug-looking brown felt hat, left to take care of itself while the owner conversed with elaborate cheerfulness to some "poor fellow" upstairs. I had just given this innocuous headgear a tremendous kick and was in the middle of a guffaw when I turned and saw Rivers standing just inside the door with a heavy bag in his hand. He was just back from leave. The memory of this little episode brings me a living picture of him, slightly different from his usual self. A spontaneous remembrance of Rivers would reveal him alert and earnest in the momentum of some discussion. (When walking he moved very fast, talking hard, and often seeming forgetful that he was being carried along by his own legs.) Standing there in the failing light of that watery afternoon, he had the half-shy look of a middle-aged person intruding on the segregative amusements of the young. For a moment he re-

garded me with an unreprimanding smile. Then he remarked, "Go steady with that hat, Sherston," and went
rapidly along the corridor to his workroom.

The hat, as I picked it up and restored its contours to
their normal respectability, looked somehow as though it
might have belonged to Doctor Macamble.

III

I have previously remarked that I would give a good deal
for a few gramophone records of my "interchanges of
ideas" with Rivers. I now reiterate the remark because at
the moment of writing I feel very much afraid of reporting
our confabulations incorrectly. In later years, while mud-
dling on toward maturity, I have made it my business to
find out all I can about the mechanism of my spontaneous
behaviour; but I cannot be sure how far I had advanced in
that art—or science—in 1917. I can only suggest that my
definite approach to mental maturity began with my contact with the mind of Rivers.

If he were alive I could not be writing so freely about
him. I might even be obliged to call him by some made-up
name, which would seem absurd. But he has been dead
nearly fourteen years now and he exists only in vigilant
and undiminished memories, continuously surviving in
what he taught me. It is that intense survival of his human
integrity which has made me pause perplexed. Can I hope
to pass the test of that invisible presence, that mind which
was devoted to the service of exact and organized research?
What exactitude would he find in such a representation of
psychological experience as this, and how far would he ap-
prove my attempt to describe him? Well, I can only trust
that he would smile at my mistakes and decide that I am
tolerably accurate about the essentials of the story.

Of one thing, at any rate, I can be certain.

In 1917 the last thing he expected me to be capable of
saying to him was—"Such knowledge as I have of the why
and wherefore of this War is only enough to make me feel

that I know nothing at all." He would have said it of himself, though, since he was merely a plain scientist, and not
an omniscient politician or political writer. And he would
have added that it pained him deeply to feel that he was
"at war" with German scientists. (At that time I did not
know that he had studied at Heidelberg.)

As regards the "larger aspects" of the War, my method
was to parade such scraps of information as I possessed,
always pretending to know more than I did. Even Rivers
could not cure me of the youthful habit (which many
people never unlearn at all) of being conversationally dis-
honest. All he could do was to make me feel uncomfortable
when I thought about it afterwards—which was, anyhow,
a step in the right direction. For instance he would be saying something about the Franco-Prussian War, and I
would bluff my way through, pretending to know quite a
lot about the Alsace-Lorraine question (though all I knew
was that I'd once been introduced to a prebendary called
Loraine, who subsequently became a canon, and who had
prepared Aunt Evelyn for confirmation somewhere about
the year 1870). Worse still, I would talk about some well-
known person as if I knew him quite well instead of having
only met him once. Since then I have entirely altered my
procedure, and when in doubt I pretend to know less than
I really do. The knowledge thus gained is part of my in-
debtedness to Rivers.

* * *

In 1917 it did not occur to me that golf would one day
be regarded as a predominant national occupation rather
than a pastime. Nevertheless I did not like the game to be
treated with levity; in fact I played it somewhat seriously.
(My friend Cromlech had once insisted on trying to defeat
me in a game in which he used nothing but a niblick; and
to my great annoyance he performed such astonishing feats
with it as to cause me some disquietude, though I won
quite comfortably in the end.)

When played seriously, even golf can, I suppose, claim
to be "an epitome of human life". Anyhow, in that fourth

October of the War I was a better golfer than I'd ever been before—and, I may add, a better one than I've ever been since.

I must admit, though, that I wasn't worrying much about the War when I'd just hit a perfect tee-shot up the charming vista which was the fairway to the first green at Mortonhall. How easy it felt! I scarcely seemed to be gripping the club at all. Afternoon sunshine was slanting through the golden-brown beeches and at last I knew what it was like to hit the ball properly. "I suppose I'm getting too keen on the game," I thought, as I bicycled home to the hydro at the end of some such afternoon, when I'd been sampling one of the delightfully unfrequented links which the War had converted into Arcadian solitudes. It was all very well, but this sort of thing couldn't go on for ever. Sooner or later I must let Rivers know my intentions. Had I been an ordinary patient I should have been due for a medical board long before now, and even Rivers couldn't postpone it indefinitely. And if I were to refuse to go before a board the situation would become awkward again. He had allowed me to drift on for twelve weeks, and so far he hadn't asked me what I intended to do or put the slightest pressure on me about it. Now that he was back from leave he would probably tackle the question. Perhaps he would do so that very evening.

Meanwhile I went up to my room and sat there cleaning my clubs. After a bit the Theosophist came in to smarten himself up before going into Edinburgh for dinner. When in good spirits he had a habit of addressing me in literary language, usually either tags of Shakespeare or locutions reminiscent of Rider Haggard's romances. If I remarked that the way the windows rattled and creaked was enough to keep one awake all night, he would reply, "True, O King," or "Thou hast uttered wise words, O great white chief." He now informed me, while rubbing his face with a towel, that he had been engaged on "enterprises of great pith and moment".

"To-day, toward the going down of the sun, O Sherston, the medicine men put forth their powers upon me, and soothfully I say unto you, they have passed me for permanent home service." Where would he go to, I enquired.

"I shall sit in an office, O man of little faith, wearing blue tabs upon my tunic and filling in Army Forms whereof no man knoweth the mysterious meaning," he replied, and left me wondering what occupation I ought to find for my disillusioned self.

* * *

Writing about it so long afterwards, one is liable to forget that while the War was going on nobody really knew when it would stop. For ordinary infantry officers like myself there was always what we called "a faint bloody hope that it may be over in six months from now". And at Slateford there was always a suppressed awareness which reminded me that I was "shortening the War" for myself every week that I remained there. No one but an expert humbug would now deny that some such awareness existed in most of us who were temporarily "out of it" but destined sooner or later to find ourselves in a front-line trench again.

While I continued to clean my clubs, some inward monitor became uncomfortably candid and remarked "This heroic gesture of yours—'making a separate peace'—is extremely convenient for you, isn't it? Doesn't it begin to look rather like dodging the Kaiser's well-aimed projectiles?" Proper pride also weighed in with a few well-chosen words. "Twelve weeks ago you may have been a man with a message. Anyhow you genuinely believed yourself to be one. But unless you can prove to yourself that your protest is still effective, you are here under false pretences, merely skrimshanking snugly along on what you did in the belief that you would be given a bad time for doing it."

Against this I argued that, having pledged myself to an uncompromising attitude, I ought to remain consistent to the abstract idea that the War was wrong. Intellectual sobriety was demanded of me. But the trouble was that I wasn't an "intellectual" at all; I was only trying to become one. I was also, it seemed, trying to become a good golfer. Rivers had never played golf in his life, though he ap-

proved of it as a healthy recreation. It would mean nothing
to him if I told him that I'd been round North Berwick in
one under bogey (which I hadn't done). There were many
other subjects we could discuss, of course, but after the first
six weeks or so there had seemed less and less to be said
about my "mental position". And it was no use pretending that I'd come to Slateford to talk to him about contemporary novelists or even the incalculability of European
Chancelleries. Sooner or later he would ask me straight out
what I intended to do. My own reticence on the subject
had been caused by the fact that I hadn't known what I
did intend to do.

I was now trying to find out, while rubbing away, with
oil and sandpaper, at an obstinate patch of rust on my
niblick. . . .

At this point in my cogitations there was a commotion of
thudding feet along the passage past my door, and I heard
a nurse saying, "Now, now, you mustn't get upset like
this." The sound of someone sobbing like a child receded
and became inaudible after the shutting of a door. That
sort of thing happened fairly often at the hydro. Men who
had "done their bit in France" crying like children. One
took it for granted, of course; but how much longer could I
stay there among so many haunted faces and "functional
nervous disorders"? Outwardly normal though a lot of
them were, it wasn't an environment which stimulated
one's "intellectual sobriety"!

I felt in my pocket for a little talisman which I always
carried about with me. It was a lump of fire-opal clasped
on a fine gold chain. Someone whose friendship I valued
highly had given it to me when I went to France and I
used to call it "my pocket sunset".

I had derived consolation from its marvellous colours
during the worst episodes of my war experiences. In its
small way it had done its best to mitigate much squalor
and despondency. My companions in dismal dug-outs had
held it in their hands and admired it.

I could not see its fiery colours now, for the room was
almost dark.

But it brought back the past in which I had made it an emblem of successful endurance, and set up a mood of reverie about the old Front Line, which really did feel as if it had been a better place than this where I now sat in bitter safety surrounded by the wreckage and defeat of those who had once been brave.

Had I really enjoyed those tours of trenches up in the Bois Français sector? For it was that period, before the Somme battles began, which now seemed to have acquired an insidious attractiveness. No; in their reality I had intensely disliked those times—except, perhaps, the excitement of my night-patrols. It hadn't been much fun when we relieved the Manchesters—sploshing and floundering up "the Old Kent Road" at midnight; posting the sentries and machine-gunners and that bombing-post at the end of the sap; taking over the familiar desolation of soggy fire-steps and sniped-at parapets and looking out again across that nothing-on-earth-like region beyond the tangled thickets of wire. And then diving under the gas-blanket in the doorway of our dug-out and groping down the steps to find Barton sitting moodily at the table with his bottle of whisky, worrying over his responsibilities while his batman cooked him some toasted cheese in the smoky recess which served as a kitchen. Up there we had arrived at the edge of the world and everything pleasant was far behind us. To be dozing doggedly on the mud-caked sandbags of a wire-netting bunk, with bits of chalk falling on one's face, was something achieved for King and Country, but it wasn't enjoyable. There was no sense, I thought, in allowing oneself to sentimentalize the smells of chloride of lime and dead rats, or in idealizing the grousings of Ormand and Mansfield because the jam ration was usually inferior, seldom Hartley's, and never Crosse and Blackwell's. But we'd all done our best to help one another, and it was good to remember Durley coming in with one of his wryfaced stories about a rifle-grenade exploding on the parados a few yards away from him—Durley demonstrating just how he'd dodged it, and creating an impression that it had been quite a funny German practical joke. Yes, we'd all of us managed to make jokes—mostly family jokes—for a company could be quite a happy family party until someone got killed. Cheerfulness under bad conditions was by no means the least heroic element of the war. Wonderful indeed had been that whimsical fortitude of the men who accepted an intense bombardment as all in the day's work and then grumbled because their cigarette ration was one packet short! But C Company Mess, as it was in the first half of 1916, could never be reassembled. Its ingredients were now imbued with ghostliness. Mansfield and Durley were disabled by wounds, and Ormand was dead. Barton was the only one of us who was functioning at the front now; he'd gone back last spring and had survived the summer and autumn without getting a scratch. Poor old devil, I thought, he must be qualifying for a spell at Slateford by now, for he'd been out there eighteen months before he was wounded the first time. . . . No, there wasn't much sense in feeling exiled from a family party which had ceased to exist; and the Bois Français sector itself had become ancient history, as remote and obsolete as the first winter of the War. Everything would be different if I went back to France now—different even from what it was last April. Gas was becoming more and more of a problem—one might almost say, more of a nightmare. Hadn't I just spent an afternoon playing golf with a man who'd lost half his company in a gas-bombardment a couple of months ago? . . . It seems to amount to this, I ruminated, twirling my putter as I polished its neck—that I'm exiled from the troops as a whole rather than from my former fellow-officers and men. And I visualized an endless column of marching soldiers, singing "Tipperary" on their way up from the back-areas; I saw them filing silently along ruined roads, and lugging their bad boots through mud until they came to some shell-hole and pillar-box line in a landscape where trees were stumps and skeletons and no Quartermaster on earth could be certain of getting the rations up. . . . "From sunlight to the sunless land". . . . The idea of going back there was indeed like death.

I suppose I ought to have concluded my strenuous wool-gatherings by adding that death is preferable to dishonour. But I didn't. Humanity asserted itself in the form of a sulky little lapse into exasperation against the people who pitied my "wrong-headedness" and regarded me as "not quite normal". In their opinion it was quite right that I should be safely out of it and "being looked after". How else could I get my own back on them but by returning to the trenches? Killed in action in order to confute the Under-Secretary for War, who had officially stated that I wasn't responsible for my actions. What a truly glorious death for a promising young pacifist! . . .

By these rather peculiar methods I argued it out with myself in the twilight. And when the windows were dark and I could see the stars, I still sat there with my golf bag between my knees, alone with what now seemed an irrefutable assurance that going back to the War as soon as possible was my only chance of peace.

*　　　　*　　　　*

As I went along to see Rivers that evening I felt rather as if I were about to make a grand gesture. I may even have felt like doing it in the grand manner. Anyhow I was full of bottled-up emotion and conscious of the significance of the occasion. Looking back from to-day, however, I am interested, not in what my own feelings were, but in what Rivers had been thinking about the decision which he had left me so entirely free to make. Had he been asked, he would probably have replied, in his driest manner, that he considered it to be his duty, as an army medical officer, to "cure me of my pacifist errors" (though one of our jokes had been about the humorous situation which would arise if I were to convert him to my point of view). Whatever he had been thinking while away on leave, he was there, with his gentle assurance of helpfulness, and all my grand gesture exuberance faded out at once. It was impossible not to be natural with Rivers. All I knew was that he was my father-confessor, as I called him, and that at last I really had got something to tell him which wasn't merely a discursive amplification of my "marking time for a few weeks" policy. As a "lead-up" to a more definite disclosure I began by telling him about the odd experience I'd had during the night before he went on leave. I knew that he was scientifically sceptical about psychic phenomena, so I laid stress on the fact that it was probably a visual delusion caused by thinking about the Western Front in stormy weather. Though I described it diffidently, the strong emotion underlying my narrative must have been apparent. But I was so full of myself and my new-made determination that I was quite surprised when I saw that my story had affected him strongly, and that it had caused him to remove his spectacles and rub them rather more than was necessary. He said little, however, and waited for me to continue. With a bumping heart I asked him what would happen if I persisted in my pacifist attitude.

"You will be kept here until the end of the War," he replied quietly. I then asked what would happen if I went before a board for reconsideration of my "mental condition". "I could only tell them that you are not suffering from any form of psycho-neurosis," he answered, adding that if I asked for permanent home service I should probably get it. I then overheard myself—as though I were a third person in the room—saying, rather hurriedly and not at all in the grand manner, "I was getting things into focus a bit while you were away and I see now that the only thing for me to do is to get back to the front as quick as I can. But what worries me is that I'm afraid of the War Office doing me down somehow and shunting me off on to some home-service job, and if I can't be passed for G.S. I won't be passed for anything at all." I could see that he was pleased; but he said that I must think it over and make quite sure that I meant it. We could then discuss our plan of campaign to wangle things with the War Office.

(He didn't actually use the word "wangle", but he implied that it might not be altogether easy to "work it" for me.) We then talked for a bit about other things and did our best to forget that there was a war on.

IV

My previous chapter began with a little exordium on the needfulness for exactitude when one is remembering and writing down what occurred a decade or two ago. At the present moment I am—to be exact—exactly 936 weeks away from my material; but that sort of accuracy is, of course, merely a matter of chronological arithmetic. Since what I am about to relate is only an interlude, I propose to allow my fantasies more freedom than is my conscientious habit. Don't assume, though, that I am about to describe something which never happened at all. Were I to do that I should be extending the art of reminiscence beyond its prescribed purpose, which is, in my case, to show myself as I am now in relation to what I was during the War.

Allow yourself then to imagine that the before-mentioned 936 weeks have not yet intervened between "now" and the autumn of 1917. You will at once observe what I can only call "one George Sherston" going full speed up a hill on the outskirts of Edinburgh. The reason for his leg-loco-motive velocity is that he is keeping pace with that quick walker, W. H. R. Rivers. The clocks of Edinburgh are an-nouncing the hour of "One" (which we shall, I fear, some day be obliged by law to call "Thirteen", though I myself intend, for an obvious reason, to compromise by referring to it as "12A"). Up that hill we go, talking (and walking) as hard as we can. For we, a couple of khaki-clad figures in (do you doubt my veracity?) "the mellow rays of an Octo-ber sun", are on our way to have luncheon with an astro-nomer; and not an ordinary astronomer either, since this one was—to put it plainly—none other than the Astro-nomer Royal of Scotland. That, so far, was all I knew and all I needed to know, my ignorance of astronomy being what it was. Rivers was taking me up there, and it pro-mised to be a very agreeable outing, and quite a contrast to that Mecca of psycho-neuroses, Slateford War Hospital.

*   *   *

Anybody who desires to verify my observations on the observatory is—or ought to be—at liberty to go there and see it for himself. But it will be one-sided verification, since I am unable to visualize, even vaguely, the actual observatory. Let us therefore assume it to be a building in all respects worthy of the lofty investigations which were why it was there—or, if you prefer it, "to which it was dedicated". Arrival and admittance having followed one another in accordance with immemorial usage, the Astronomer Royal welcomed us with the cordiality of a man who has plenty to spare for his fellow-men—no cordiality being required of him by the constellations, comets, and other self-luminous bodies which he had spent so much of his time in scrutinizing. I have known people who would probably have improvised some such conversational opening as "Well, sir, and how are the stars? Any new ones lately?"—but I was too shy to say anything at all to a man so widely acquainted with the universe. We were introduced to the fourth member of the quartet, a jocular-looking parson who rejoiced in the name of Father Rosary, and was, I inferred, a priest. We then sat down to luncheon. As I glanced around the room, which had eighteenth-century charm, I no longer felt shy and was completely prepared to enjoy myself. This feeling may have been brought on by Father Rosary, who was evidently an artist at creating a pleasant impression and following it up by being the best possible company. What did he talk about, I wonder, during that luncheon which has now become a memory of indistinct delightfulness—as all such luncheons should?

He told us amusing stories; witty stories, well worth remembering; but I have forgotten them. He spoke of entrancing places in foreign countries; but I had never seen them and they were only names which made me wish I'd been less unenterprising, instead of waiting for a European war to transport me abroad. He talked, without ostentation, about famous people whom he'd known. Who were they, I wonder? I rather think he mentioned Walter Pater (whose cadenced prose I had read with more awareness of

its music than of its instructive ingredients) and if he didn't,
he ought to have done. There was indeed an untranslat-
ably Paterish quality about Father Rosary when he was
being eloquently urbane. I suppose one should call it "an
aroma of humanism"—which means that his religious
vocation had not prevented him from being helpfully interested in everything that men think and do.

He was, so to speak, a connoisseur in the wisdom of the
ages, and I can imagine his rich voice rolling out that fine
passage of Pater's which cannot be quoted too often: "For
the essence of humanism is that belief of which he seems
never to have doubted, that nothing which has ever interested living men and women can wholly lose its vitality—
no language they have spoken, nor oracle beside which they
have hushed their voices, no dream which has once been
entertained by actual human minds, nothing about which
they have ever been passionate, or expended time and zeal."

Meanwhile our lively host had uncorked a bottle of ancient champagne. It might be a century old, he said, or it
might be less. But it was probably the most absurdly obsolete bottle of champagne in Edinburgh, and might, he
added, be a bit insipid. He had discovered it in his cellar;
some previous astronomer had left it there, and by miracu-
lous oversight it had survived to be sniffed and inspected
by Father Rosary and finally subjected to the tasting test
of his impeccable palate for wine. Rivers, who was a good
judge of water, sipped it respectfully and (after admiring
the delicate old glass from which it was fulfilling its destiny
by being at last imbibed) remarked that he'd never tasted
anything like it in his life. Father Rosary commented on its
"solemn stillness", and then, he alone knew why, began
talking about Tennyson. "Do you young men read Tennyson?" he asked me, and quoted "Now sleeps the crimson
petal, now the white" with the subdued relish of an epi-
cure. The astronomer, however, hadn't much use for
poetry. Astronomy made it seem a bit unnecessary, he
thought. "*Now slides the silent meteor on*—pretty enough—
but if he'd known what I do about meteors he wouldn't
have put it into a poem."

"But I thought he took a great interest in astronomy," I ventured.

"Yes; but he used it to suit his own game of idealizing the universe, and never really faced those ghastly immensities I'm always staring at," he replied, revealing for a moment the "whatever brute or blackguard made the world" outlook which showed itself in his face when he wasn't cracking jokes with Father Rosary, whose personality seemed to imply that Heaven was an invisible Vatican, complete with library, art-collection, and museum. Rivers, who wasn't a great poetry reader (he was handicapped by having no visual memory) remarked that he had an indistinct recollection of some poem by Tennyson in which he had to some extent "seen eye to eye" with the astronomer. There was no copy of Tennyson's works up at the observatory, but had we consulted one we should have found that Rivers was right. The line "These are Astronomy and Geology, terrible Muses" can scarcely be classed as an idealization of those two realities.

Father Rosary now recreated harmonious gaiety by seating himself at the piano and trolling out a series of delightful ditties. After that he led us yet further from uncomfortable controversies by playing some classical and nobly serious pieces, for he loved the old Italian masters. And when, at the final chords, I looked across the room, the ultimate serenity of the music seemed to be at rest in the face of my friend.

V

Sitting myself down at the table to resume this laborious task after twenty-four hours' rest, I told myself that I was "really feeling fairly fresh again". And I could have sworn that I heard the voice of Rivers say "Good!" I mention this just to show the way my mind works, though I suppose one ought not to put that sort of "aside" into a book, especially as I am always reminding myself to be ultra-careful to keep my story "well inside the frame". But I begin to feel as if I were inside the frame myself, and that being so, I don't see why Rivers shouldn't be inside it too—in more ways than one.

Well—to continue the chronicle—there were moments, after I'd emerged from my anti-war imbroglio (forgive the phrase, it amuses me) when I felt not unnaturally upset at the idea of returning to the good old trenches, though I did what I could to sublimate that "great adventure" into something splendid. The whole business was now safely settled and the date of my medical board was early in November. Rivers had made an expedition to London on my behalf, had interviewed two influential personages, and had obtained the required guarantee that no obstacles would be placed in my road back to regions where bombs, mustard-gas, box-barrages, and similar enjoyments were awaiting me.

He showed me a letter from one of them (a devoted "public servant" with whom I'd often played cricket in the old days, and whom no one but a maniac could possibly have disliked) in which the writer referred to me (in collaboration with his typist) as "our poor friend", which thereafter became our favourite term for alluding to me.

In weaker moments, as I said before, "our poor friend" somewhat bleakly realized what he had let himself in for, and, without actually wishing he hadn't done it, felt an irrepressible hankering for some sort of reprieve. Since mid-October mental detachment had been made easier by my having been given a small room to myself—an insidious privilege which allowed me to ruminate without interruption. Bad weather prevented me from playing golf all day and every day, and my brain became more active in the evenings. I spent ambrosial hours with favourite authors, and a self-contained, "dug-in" state of mind ensued.

My temperamental tendency to day-dreaming asserted itself and I realized how much I craved for solitude and mental escape from my surroundings.

When cold weather came I was allowed a scuttle of coal and could lie in bed watching the firelight flickering on the walls and the embers glowing in the grate. On such nights I remembered untroubled days and idealized my childhood, returning to the times when I was recovering from some illness and could dwell in realms of reverie, as when one surrenders to the spell of a book which evokes summers long ago and people transmuted by the author's mind to happy phantoms. Imagination recreated Aunt Evelyn reading aloud to me—her voice going lullingly on and on with one of R. L. Stevenson's stories, until she decided that it was time for some more medicine, for she was fond of amateur doctoring, and soon she would be busy with the medicine dropper, preparing one of her homeopathic remedies. Now I come to think of it, Aunt Evelyn's world was divided into "Homeopats" and "Allopats", who were much the same as Conservatives and Liberals; and the "Allopats" were in the same category as Radicals in whom no virtue resided. In other words, my reveries went back to the beginning of these memoirs, living them over again until August 1914 pulled me up short.

This was a permissible self-indulgence, for the past was still there to be used as a sedative in discreet doses—three drops in half a wine glass of water, so to speak. Looking at the future was quite a different matter.

There had been times since I came to Slateford when I had, rather guardedly, given myself a glimpse of an *après la guerre* existence, but I hadn't done any cosy day-dreaming about it. My talks with Rivers had increased my awareness of the limitations of my pre-war life. He had shown that he believed me to be capable of achieving something useful. He had set me on the right road and made me feel that if the War were to end to-morrow I should be starting on a new life's journey in which point-to-point races and cricket matches would no longer be supremely important and a strenuous effort must be made to take some small share in the real work of the world.

If the War were to end to-morrow! . . . That was where I remembered that my future was unlikely to happen at all. The fireproof curtain was still lowered in front of the stage on which post-war events would be enacted; and life, with an ironic gesture, had contrived that the man who had lit up my future with a new eagerness to do well in it should now be instrumental in sending me back to an even-money chance of being killed.

Here was I, in my little room, with a fire burning brightly and a dozen of the world's literary masterpieces tidily arranged on my table. Where should I be by the end of November? I wondered; for I was expecting that, since I was such a "special case", I should be sent back without much delay. The contrast, as regards comfort, between where I was now and where I might be in a few weeks' time needed no stressing. Realizing how much I wanted not to lose that chance of a "new life", I experienced a sort of ordeal by self-immolation. Immolation for what? I asked myself. I should be returning to the War with no belief in what I was doing; I should go through with it in a spirit of loneliness and detachment because there was no alternative. Going back was the only way out of an impossible situation. At the front I should at least find forgetfulness. And I would rather be killed than survive as one who had "wangled" his way through by saying that the War ought to stop. Better to be in the trenches with those whose experience I had shared and understood than with this medley of civilians who, when one generalized about them intolerantly, seemed either being broken by the War or enriched and made important by it. Whatever the soldiers might be as individuals, they seemed a more impressive spectacle as a whole in their endurance of what was imposed on them. But then there was my freedom to be considered. After all I had been under no one's orders lately, and at the best of times a platoon commander's life was just one damned thing after another. It's got to be done, I thought. That was about all I'd got to keep me up to scratch, and I went through some fairly murky moments in that little room of mine. It was, in fact, not at all unlike a renunciation of life and all that it had to offer me. As regards being dead, however, one of my main consolations has always been that I have the strongest intention of being an extremely active ghost. Let nobody make any mistake about that.

*   *   *

It must have been just before my medical board was due to take place that the great administrative crisis occurred at Slateford. The details of this event were as follows. The commandant (or head doctor) who had won the gratitude and affection of everyone whose opinion was worth anything, was duly notified, several weeks in advance, that the chief medical mandarin from the War Office would inspect the hospital. This, of course, signified automatically that elaborate efforts must be made to ensure that he should see Slateford as it had never been before and never would be again. The spit and polish process should, I suppose, have been applied even to the patients, on whom it was incumbent that they should be looking their best. "Always remember that you belong to the smartest shell-shock hospital in the British Army" should have been the order of the day.

But the commandant had his own ideas about eyewash, and he decided that the general should, just for once, see a war hospital as it really was.

He did this as a matter of principle, since in his opinion a shell-shock hospital was not the same thing as a parade ground. But administrative inspectorship failed to see the point of that sort of thing, and the mandarin was genuinely shocked by what he inspected. He went into the kitchen and found that he couldn't see his face reflected in a single frying-pan. You couldn't eat your dinner off the bathroom floors, and Sam Browne belts were conspicuous by their absence. Worst of all, most of the medical staff were occupied with their patients, instead of standing about and wasting their time for an hour or two while awaiting the arrival of their supreme therapeutic war-lord. Profoundly displeased, he departed. The place was a disgrace, and only showed what happened when civilians in uniform were allowed to run a war hospital in their own way. The commandant was notified that someone else would take over his commandancy, and the rest of the staff sent in their resignations as a demonstration of loyalty to him. These after-effects, as far as I can remember, were as yet unknown to the patients. Had I been aware that Rivers would soon be leaving the hospital I am sure I should not have done the very stupid thing which I am about to describe.

*   *   *

There are two ways of telling a good story well—the quick way and the slow way. Personally I prefer a good story to be told slowly. What I am about to tell is not a good story. It is merely an episode which cannot be left out. A certain abruptness is therefore appropriate.

On the appointed afternoon I smartened myself up and waited to be called before the medical board. I was also going to tea with the astronomer, who had promised to let me have a look at the moon through his telescope. But I was feeling moody and irritable, and I had to wait my turn, which was a long time in coming. Gradually I became petulant and impatient. After an hour and a half I looked at my watch for the last time, said to myself that the medical board could go to blazes, and then (I record it with regret) went off to have tea with the astronomer. It was one of those self-destructive impulses which cause people, in sheer cussedness, to do things which are to their own disadvantage. I suddenly felt "fed up with being mucked about by the War"—as I should have expressed it—and forgot all about Rivers and everything that I owed him.

Seeking some explanation of my behaviour I have wondered whether I was feeling ill without being aware of it. But I don't remember developing an influenza-cold afterwards; and if I did it would have been a poorish excuse.

In these days of incalculable dictators, by the way, (and in my humble opinion the proper place for a dictator is a parenthesis) one cannot help wondering whether an acute Continental crisis could not quite conceivably be caused by an oncoming chill. May I therefore be allowed to suggest that before hurling explosive ultimatums, all dictators should be persuaded to have their temperatures taken. One pictures the totalitarian tyrant with fountain-pen poised above some imperious edict, when the human touch intervenes in the form of a trained nurse-secretary (also a dead shot with a revolver) who slips a thermometer into

that ever-open mouth. One figures him, with eyes dyna-
mically dilated, breathing stertorously through the nose
during this test of his sense of supreme responsibility for the
well-being of the world. . . . "Just half a minute more, to
make quite sure". . . . With a bright smile she hands the
tiny talisman to a gravely-expectant medicine man, who,
it may be, shakes his head and murmurs, "Nine-nine point
nine. Your Supremacy should sign no documents till to-
morrow morning." Poof! What a relief for Europe! . . .

To return to my insignificant self: before I was half-way
to Edinburgh on the top of a tram I realized that I had
done something unthinkably foolish. But it was too late
now. The stars looked down on me, and soon I should be
making the most of them through the largest telescope in
Scotland. But the document which might have a conclu-
sive effect on my earthly career was still unsigned.

Of my tea with the astronomer, I only remember that he
couldn't get the telescope to work properly. He pushed and
pulled, swivelled it and swore at it, and finally gave it up
as a bad job. So even the moon was a washout. Downstairs
he took me into a darkened room and showed me a delicate instrument which I can only describe by saying that it
contained a small blob of luminosity, which was, I rather
think, radium. What was the instrument for? I asked. He
told me that it was used for measuring infinitesimal frac-
tions of a second. He then explained how it did it.

*   *   *

Rivers, as I have already attempted to indicate, was a
wonderful man. He certainly made me aware of it after I'd
offered him my wretched explanation. It was, thank heaven, the only time I ever saw him seriously annoyed with
me. As might be expected, he looked not only annoyed,
but stern. The worst part was that he looked thoroughly
miserable. With averted eyes I mumbled out my story;
how I'd lost my temper because I was kept waiting; how I
really didn't know why I'd done it; and how it was nothing
to do with backing out of my decision to give up being a
pacifist. When he heard this his face changed. He looked

relieved. My eyes met his; and when I dolefully exclaimed "And now I suppose I've dished the whole thing, just through having said I'd go to tea with the astronomer!" he threw his head back and laughed in that delightful way of his. For me it was about the best laugh he ever indulged in, for it meant that he'd put the whole board-cutting business behind him and was ready to repair the damage without delay. Not a word of reproach did he utter. I was causing him a lot of extra trouble, but he merely remarked that he might find some difficulty in getting my papers past the new commandant, whose arrival was imminent. This officer was believed to be ultra-conventional in his ideas about the mental deportment of young officers, and it was feared that his attitude toward the psychoses would be somewhat adamantine. Whether it really was adamantine I am unable to say, for I don't seem to remember much about those three weeks which concluded my career at Slateford.

Oddly enough, the agitation created by board-cutting produced an ableptical effect on my introspectiveness. The episode provided a sort of bridge between psychological disquietude and a calm acceptance of "the inevitable". In other words, I ceased to worry.

When—at the end of that period of which I can only remember that I wanted it to be over quickly—I was actually waiting to go in and "be boarded", I felt self-confident but a little nervous about the result. My cranium, however, contained nothing definite except the first two lines of "Locksley Hall". (Something similar had happened when I was being "boarded" at Liverpool the previous July.) "*Comrades, leave me here a little, while as yet 'tis early morn*" (it was after lunch, and I was reclining on a dingy red plush sofa in the lofty but depressing saloon). "*Leave me here, and when you want me blow upon the bugle-horn*" ... What was the connection? Was it because they'd talked about Tennyson up at the observatory, or was "Locksley Hall" something to do with being under lock and key, or was it merely because the bugle-horn was about to blow me back to the army? One thing was obvious, at any rate. I must not ask the medical board to solve this enigma for

me. When the moment arrived for me to take a deep breath
and step discreetly in, I found Rivers looking as solemn as
a judge, sitting at a table where he'd been telling the other
two as much of my case as he deemed good for them. In a
manner which was, I hoped, a nice blend of deference and
self-assurance, I replied to a few perfunctory questions
about my health. There was a fearsome moment when the
commandant picked up my "dossier"; but Rivers diverted
his attention with some remark or other and he put the
papers down again. The commandant looked rather as if
he wanted his tea. I was then duly passed for general service abroad—an event which seldom happened from Slateford. But that was not all. Without knowing it, two-thirds
of the medical board had restored me to my former status.
I was now "an officer and a gentleman", again.

*   *   *

Next morning I had my last look at the hydro before
departing to entrain for Liverpool. Feeling no inclination
to request my comrades to leave me there a little, I became
quite certain that I never wanted to see the place again.

I had said good-bye to Rivers. Shutting the door of his
room for the last time, I left behind me someone who had
helped and understood me more than anyone I had ever
known. Much as he disliked speeding me back to the
trenches, he realized that it was my only way out. And the
longer I live the more right I know him to have been.

And now, before conveying myself away from Slateford,
I must add a few final impressions. The analysis and inter-
pretation of dreams was an important part of the work
which Rivers did; and, as everyone ought to know, his con-
tributions to that insubstantial field of investigation were
extremely valuable.

About my own dreams he hadn't bothered much, but as
there may be someone who needs to be convinced that I
wasn't suffering from shell-shock, I am offering a scrap of
dream evidence, which for all I know may prove that I
was!

Since the War I have experienced two distinct and re-

current specimens of war-dream. Neither of them expressed
any dislike of high-explosive. I have never had nightmares
about being shelled, though I must confess to a few recent
ones about being bombed from the air, but that was probably caused by reading the newspapers.

The two recurrent dreams were, (1): I was with my battalion in some slough of despond, from which it seemed
there was no way back. We were all doomed to perish in
the worst possible of all most hopeless "dud shows". Our
only enemy was mud. This was caused by hearing about
the Ypres salient, and by the haunting fear that sooner or
later I should find myself in some such "immortal morass",
as it might be designated by one of those lofty-minded persons who prefer to let bygones be bygones—one might call
them "the Unknown Warrior School of Unrealists"—
"these men perished miserably, but the spirit in which they
did it lives for ever", and so on. Measured in terms of unmitigated horror, this dream was, I think, quite good peace
propaganda. But the queer thing about it was that while in
the thick of my dream-despair, I sometimes thought "Anyhow I am adding a very complete piece of war experience
to my collection". This dream did not recur after I had
written my account of military service.

The second dream still recurs, every two or three months.
It varies in context and background, but always amounts
to the same thing. The War is still going on and I have got
to return to the front. I complain bitterly to myself because
it hasn't stopped yet. I am worried because I can't find my
active-service kit. I am worried because I have forgotten
how to be an officer. I feel that I can't face it again, and
sometimes I burst into tears and say "It's no good. I can't
do it." But I know that I can't escape going back, and
search frantically for my lost equipment.

Sometimes I actually find myself "out there" (though
the background is always in England—the Germans have
usually invaded half Kent). And, as in the first dream, I
am vaguely gratified at "adding to my war experience".
I take out a patrol and am quite keen about it.

This dream obviously dates from the autumn of 1917,

when I made the choice which seemed like a "potential death-sentence". If it proves anything it is this; the fact that it was everybody's business to be prepared to die for his country did not alter the inward and entirely personal grievance one had against being obliged to do it. The instinct of self-preservation automatically sank below all arguments put forward by one's "higher self". "I don't want to die," it insisted. "I want to be a middle-aged man writing memoirs, and not a 'glorious name' living for evermore on a block of stone subject to the inevitable attritions and obfuscations caused by climate." "But your deathless name will be invisibly inscribed in the annals of your imperishable race" argued some celestial leader-writer. "I prefer to peruse to-morrow's *Times* in normal decrepitude" replied ignoble self-preservation.

*   *   *

It would be an exaggeration if I were to describe Slateford as a depressing place by daylight. The doctors did everything possible to counteract gloom, and the wrecked faces were outnumbered by those who were emerging from their nervous disorders. But the War Office had wasted no money on interior decoration; consequently the place had the melancholy atmosphere of a decayed hydro, redeemed only by its healthy situation and pleasant view of the Pentland Hills. By daylight the doctors dealt successfully with these disadvantages, and Slateford, so to speak, "made cheerful conversation".

But by night they lost control and the hospital became sepulchral and oppressive with saturations of war experience. One lay awake and listened to feet padding along passages which smelt of stale cigarette-smoke; for the nurses couldn't prevent insomnia-ridden officers from smoking half the night in their bedrooms, though the locks had been removed from all doors. One became conscious that the place was full of men whose slumbers were morbid and terrifying—men muttering uneasily or suddenly crying out in their sleep. Around me was that underworld of dreams haunted by submerged memories of warfare and its intolerable shocks and self-lacerating failures to achieve the impossible. By daylight each mind was a sort of aquarium for the psychopath to study. In the daytime, sitting in a sunny room, a man could discuss his psycho-neurotic symptoms with his doctor, who could diagnose phobias and conflicts and formulate them in scientific terminology. Significant dreams could be noted down, and Rivers could try to remove repressions. But by night each man was back in his doomed sector of a horror-stricken Front Line, where the panic and stampede of some ghastly experience was re-enacted among the livid faces of the dead. No doctor could save him then, when he became the lonely victim of his dream disasters and delusions.

Shell-shock. How many a brief bombardment had its long-delayed after-effect in the minds of these survivors, many of whom had looked at their companions and laughed while inferno did its best to destroy them. Not then was their evil hour, but now; now, in the sweating suffocation of nightmare, in paralysis of limbs, in the stammering of dislocated speech. Worst of all, in the disintegration of those qualities through which they had been so gallant and selfless and uncomplaining—this, in the finer types of men, was the unspeakable tragedy of shell-shock; it was in this that their humanity had been outraged by those explosives which were sanctioned and glorified by the Churches; it was thus that their self-sacrifice was mocked and maltreated—they, who in the name of righteousness had been sent out to maim and slaughter their fellow-men. In the name of civilization these soldiers had been martyred, and it remained for civilization to prove that their martyrdom wasn't a dirty swindle.

PART TWO: LIVERPOOL AND LIMERICK

I

It is not impossible that on my way back to Clitherland I compared my contemporary self with previous Sherstons who had reported themselves for duty there.

First the newly-gazetted young officer, who had yet to utter his first word of command—anxious only to become passably efficient for service at the front. (How young I had been then—not much more than two and a half years ago!) Next came the survivor of nine months in France (the trenches had taught *him* a thing or two anyhow) less diffident, and inclined, in a confused way, to ask the reason why everyone was doing and dying under such soul-destroying conditions. Thirdly arrived that somewhat incredible mutineer who had made up his mind that if a single human being could help to stop the War by making a fuss, he was that man.

There they were, those three Sherstons; and here was I —the inheritor of their dim renown. Reporting for duty again, that was all it boiled down to, after making a proper fool of myself instead of just carrying on and taking the cushy job which I could have had for the asking without anyone uttering a word against me.

Driving out to the camp in a taxi, however, I didn't doubt that I should be received with heartiness—albeit tinged with embarrassment. I must try not to think about it, I thought; and anyhow it was a comfort not to be arriving there with a bee in my bonnet; which was, I supposed, what they'd all been saying about my behaviour. But my arrival turned out to be an anti-climax. A surprise awaited me. Only a few days before, the Depot had been transplanted to Ireland on account of the troubles there. Clitherland Camp was to be taken over by an Irish battalion. In the meantime it was occupied by the Assistant-Adjutant and a few dozen "details", plus a couple of hundred recruits and men returned from hospital. So everything was quite easy. What did my concerns matter when the whole Depot had been revolutionized? The Assistant-Adjutant, who had been permanently disabled early in the War, was a much-loved institution. Warmly welcomed by him, I passed a pleasant evening discussing everything except people with pacifist opinions, and on the whole I felt quite pleased to be back inside the sheepfold.

But when I was alone—that was where the difficulty began. What was it—that semi-suicidal instinct which haunted me whenever I thought about going back to the line? Did I really feel an insidious craving to be killed, or am I only imagining it now? Was it "spiritual pride", or was it just war-weariness and repressed exasperation?

What I mean is this—that being alone with oneself is not the same thing as succeeding in being a good-natured and unpretentious person while talking to one's friends. With the Assistant-Adjutant I was "the same old Sherston as ever" —adapting himself to other people's notions and doing his best to be cheerful. But in spite of my reliance on Rivers and my resolve to remain, through his influence, sensible and unimpulsive, none the less in what, for the sake of exposition I will call my soul, (Grand Soul Theatre; performances nightly) protagonistic performances were keeping the drama alive. (I might almost say that there was a bit of "ham" acting going on at times.)

For my soul had rebelled against the War, and not even Rivers could cure it of that. To feel in some sort of way heroic—that was the only means I could devise for "carrying on". Hence, when I arrived at Clitherland, my tragedian soul was all ready to start back for the trenches with a sublime gesture of self-sacrifice. But it was an angry soul, with no inclination to be nice to anyone except its fellow-soldiers. It wanted to see itself dominating the audience (mainly civilians) and dying defiantly in some lime-lighted shell-hole; "martyred because he could not save mankind," as his platoon-sergeant remarked afterwards, in a burst of blank-verse eloquence of which he had hitherto believed himself incapable.

The Orderly Room, however, was unconscious of all this. After spending three idle days at the camp, I was instructed to proceed—not to "some corner of a foreign field"—but wherever I wanted to go during ten days' leave. I was unofficially told I could make it twelve if I liked.

*   *   *

My memories of that bit of leave are distinctly hazy. It goes without saying that the object of going on leave was to enjoy oneself. This I determined to do. I also made up my mind to be as brainless as I could, which may account for my not being able to remember much of it now, since it is only natural that the less you think about what you are doing the less there is to remember.

Butley, with its unavoidable absence of liveliness, did make me to some extent cerebrally aware of what was happening to me. Through no fault of its own, it suffered from the disadvantage of being "just the same as ever"—except that all the life seemed to have gone out of it. And I was merely my old self, on final leave, with Aunt Evelyn doing her level best to make things bright and comfortable for me. The pathos of her efforts needs no emphasizing, though thinking of it gives me a heartache, even now. A strong smell of frying onions greeted my arrival. This, anyhow, gave me a chance to say how fond I was of that odour—as indeed I still am. "Steaks are quite difficult to get now, dear, so I do hope it's a tender one,' she remarked. And afterwards, while we were eating it, "Much as it disagrees with me I never can resist the merry onion."

Her tired face was just about as merry as an onion. And the steak, of course, was tough. We hadn't much to tell one another either. Conversation about Slateford was restricted to my saying what a good place it was for golf, and there was an awkwardness even in telling her what a wonderful man Dr. Rivers was, since his name at once raised the spectre of my "protest", which neither of us desired to discuss.

No doubt she had hoped and prayed that I might get a home-service job; but now she just accepted the fact that I'd got to go out again.

Naturally, I didn't include Aunt Evelyn among the people on whom I wanted to get my own back by being killed. But I knew that she disapproved of people being pacifists when there was a war to be won. So she suffered in silence; and if I said anything at all it was probably in the "don't much care what happens to me" style which young people go in for when in contact with elderly and anxious relatives. So Aunt Evelyn had nothing to console her except her one form of optimism, which was to try and believe that the Germans were doing so badly that very soon there would be none left.

And the only news she could think of was that dear old Mrs. Hawthorn was dead, which didn't lead to anything except the fact that she had been nearly ninety. Yet if I'd heard about it when I was in my little room at Slateford I should have indulged in quite a pleasant reverie about old Mrs. Hawthorn and the children's parties I used to go to at her house, and how she used to sit there like a queen, her artificial complexion so perfectly put on that nobody minded in the least, though in a younger person it would have been thought highly improper. But that was before the Boer War, and now the "Great One" had killed both Mrs. Hawthorn's great-nephews—those handsome boys of whom she had been so proud when she gave parties for them.

Sitting here in my omniscience I am inclined to blame Aunt Evelyn and myself for not realizing that the only solution for "final leave" was to open a bottle of champagne. But there was no champagne in the house. From patriotic principles, Aunt Evelyn preferred Empire wines. (I don't wish to libel South African hock, but the vine which produced Aunt Evelyn's vintage must have been first cousin to an aloe.) Meanwhile we did our best to be communicative, and after keeping introspection at arm's length from Friday till Tuesday, I went off to Sussex and stayed with the Moffats, who knew all about opening bottles of bubbly; and there I had a couple of days with the hounds and succeeded in being authentically jolly. I can remember one good hunt along the vale below the downs. I hadn't felt so happy since I didn't know when, I thought; which merely meant that while galloping and jumping on a good horse everything else was forgotten—for forty-five minutes of the best, anyhow. And there was no sense in feeling morbid about the dead; they were well out of the war, anyway; and they wouldn't grudge me my one good day in the vale.

After that there was London with its good dinners and an air-raid and seeing a few friends and going to a few theatres, and before I knew where I was, Clitherland Camp had claimed me for its own again.

I was feeling much more cheerful, and I told myself that I intended to lead a life of light-hearted stupidity. At Slateford I had been an individual isolated from outside influences, with plenty of time for thinking things over and finding out who I was. Now I was back in the brain-fuddling existence which did its best to prevent my thinking at all. I had to knock out my pipe and go on parade. My time was no longer my own. My military duties, however, were more a matter of killing time than of using it, and we were all merely waiting to move across to Ireland. So for about three weeks after I came back from leave I was in much the same position as the man in the comic song:

I'd got lots of time to do it; but there wasn't much to do
When I was made head-keeper—of the pheasants at the Zoo.

II

While writing these memoirs, my interest in each chapter has been stimulated by the fact that I nearly always saw myself engaged in doing something for the first time. Even if it was only "going back to Butley", I wasn't quite the same as when I'd last left it, so one hoped that monotony was being avoided. All this, I suspect, has been little more

than the operation known as the pilgrimage from the cradle
to the grave, but I have had a comfortable feeling that,
however ordinary my enterprises may have been, they had
at any rate the advantage of containing, for me, an element
of sustained unfamiliarity. I am one of those persons who
begin life by exclaiming that they've "never seen anything
like it before" and die in the hope that they may say the
same of heaven.

Time has taught me that this talent for experiencing
everyday life with ever-renewed freshness and intensity is
the best qualification for making one's memoirs readable.
Professional ruminator though I admittedly am, I cannot
accuse myself of lacking interest in life, and my main difficulty has been that I absorb so much that I am continually
asking to be allowed to sit still and digest the good (and
bad) things which life has offered me. A ruminator really
needs two lives; one for experiencing and another for thinking it over. Knowing that I *need* two lives and am only
allowed one, I do my best to *lead* two lives; with the inevitable consequence that I am told by the world's busybodies
that I am "turning my back on the contemporary situation". Such people are usually so busy trying to crowd the
whole of life into their daily existence that they get very
little of it permanently inside their craniums. My own idea
is that it is better to carry the best part of one's life about in
one's head for future reference.

As the reader already knows, I have seldom gone out in
search of adventurous material. My procedure has always
been to allow things to happen to me in their own time.
The result was that when anything unexpected did happen
to me it impressed itself on my mind as being significant.
I can therefore claim that my terrestrial activities have
been either accidental in origin or else part of the "inevitable sequence of events". Had there been no Great War I
might quite conceivably have remained on English soil till
I was buried in it. Others have done the same, so why not
Sherston? The fact remains that up to the end of 1917 I
had never been to Ireland.

Outwardly it was a dismal journey, for I left Liverpool

late at night and the weather was wintry. Crewe station at midnight was positively Plutonian. Waiting for the Holyhead express to come in, I listened to echoing clangour and hissing steam; people paced the platform with fixedly dejected faces, while glaring lights and gloom and vapour intermingled above them. Crewe station and everyone inside it seemed to be eternally condemned to the task of winning the War by moving men, munitions, and material to the places appointed for them in the outer darkness of Armageddon. This much I observed as I stood with hunched-up shoulders, feeling sombrely impressed by the strangeness of the scene. Then I boarded the Holyhead train, remembering how I used to ride along the Watling Street with the Packlestone Hounds and see "Holyhead, 200 miles" on a signpost; this memory led me to wonder whether I should get a day's hunting in Ireland. After that an "inevitable sequence of events" carried me across to Dublin, and thence to Limerick. There was snow on the ground and the Emerald Isle was cold and crunchy underfoot.

          *   *   *

By the time I had been at Limerick a week I knew that I had found something closely resembling peace of mind. My body stood about for hours on parade, watching young soldiers drill and do physical training, and this made it easy for me to spend my spare time refusing to think. I felt extraordinarily healthy, and I was seldom alone. There had been no difficulty in reverting to what the people who thought they knew me would have called my "natural self". I merely allowed myself to become what they expected me to be. As someone good-naturedly remarked, I had "given up lecturing on the prevention of war-weariness"—(which meant, I suppose, that the only way to prevent it was to stop the War). The "New Barracks", which had been new for a good many years, were much more cheerful than the huts at Clitherland, and somehow made me feel less like a temporary soldier. Looking at the lit windows of the barrack square on my first evening in Ireland, I felt profoundly thankful that I wasn't at Slateford. And the curfew-tolling bells of Limerick Cathedral sounded much better than the factory hooters around Clitherland Camp. I had been talking to four officers who had been with me in the First Battalion in 1916, and we had been reviving memories of what had become the more or less good old days at Mametz. Two of them had been wounded in the Ypres battle three months before, and their experiences had apparently made Mametz Wood seem comparatively pleasant, and the "unimaginable touch of time" had completed the mellowing process.

Toward the end of my second week the frost and snow changed to soft and rainy weather. One afternoon I walked out to Adare and saw for the first time the Ireland which I had imagined before I went there. Quite unexpectedly I came in sight of a wide shallow river, washing and hastening past the ivied stones of a ruined castle among some ancient trees. The evening light touched it all into romance, and I indulged in ruminations appropriate to the scene. But this was not enough, and I soon began to make enquiries about the meets of the Limerick Hounds.

No distance, I felt, would be too great to go if only I could get hold of a decent hireling. Nobody in the barracks could tell me where to look for one. The genial majors permanent at the Depot were fond of a bit of shooting and fishing, but they had no ambition to be surmounting stone walls and big green banks with double ditches. Before long however, I had discovered a talkative dealer out at Croome, and I returned from my first day's hunting feeling that I'd had more than my money's worth. The whole thing had been most exhilarating. Everyone rode as if there wasn't a worry in the world except hounds worrying foxes. Never had I galloped over such richly verdant fields or seen such depth of blue in distant hills. It was difficult to believe that such a thing as "trouble" existed in Ireland, or that our majors were talking in apprehensive undertones about being sent out with mobile columns—the mere idea of our mellow majors going out with mobile columns seemed slightly ludicrous.

But there it was. The Irish were being troublesome—extremely troublesome—and no one knew much more than that, except that our mobile columns would probably make them worse.

Meanwhile there was abundance of real dairy butter, and I sent some across to Aunt Evelyn every week.

At the end of the third week in January my future as an Irish hunting man was conclusively foreshortened. My name came through on a list of officers ordered to Egypt. After thinking it over, I decided, with characteristic imbecility, that I would much rather go to France. I had got it fixed in my mind that I was going to France, and to be informed that I was going to Egypt instead seemed an anticlimax. I talked big to myself about Palestine being only a side-show; but I also felt that I should put up a better performance with a battalion where I was already known. So I wired to the C.O. of our second battalion asking him to try and get me posted to them; but my telegram had no result, and I heard afterwards that the C.O. had broken his leg the day after it arrived, riding along a frost-slippery street in Ypres. I don't suppose that the War Office would have posted me to him in any case; and I only record it as one of life's little contrasts—that while I was enjoying myself with the Limerick Hounds, one of our most gallant and popular senior officers—himself a fine horseman—was being put out of action while riding quietly along a road in the town which held the record for being knocked to ruins by crumps.

A day or two later, greatly to my disgust, I was despatched to Cork to attend an anti-gas course. I didn't take my studies very seriously, as I'd heard it all before and there was nothing new to learn. So on the fourth and last day I cut the exam. and had a hunt with the Muskerry Hounds. I had introduced myself to a well-known horse-dealer in Cork who hunted the hounds, and the result was that I had a nice little scramble over a rough country about eighteen miles away from the army hut where I ought to have been putting on paper such great thoughts as "gas projectors consist of drums full of liquid gas fired by trench-mortars set at an angle of forty-five degrees".

In the afternoon the hounds were drawing slowly along some woods above the river which flowed wide and rain-swollen down long glens and reaches in a landscape that was all grey-green and sad and lonely. I thought what a haunted ancient sort of land it was. It seemed to go deep into my heart while I looked at it, just as it had done when I gazed at the castle ruins at Adare.

In the county club that evening I got into conversation with a patrician-faced old parson. We were alone by the smoking-room fire, and after he'd been reminiscing de-lightfully about hunting it transpired that he had a son in the Cameronians. And I discovered that this son of his had been one of the officers in the headquarters dug-out in the Hindenburg trench while I was waiting to go up to the bombing attack in which I was wounded.

We agreed that this was a remarkable coincidence. It certainly felt like a queer little footnote to my last year's experience, and the old gentleman laughed heartily when I said to him "If life was like *Alice in Wonderland*, I suppose I should have said to your son—not 'I think I once met your father in Ireland' but 'I think in nine months' time I shall be talking to your father in the county club at Cork'." We then decided that on the whole it was just as well that the Almighty had arranged that *homo sapiens* should be denied the power of foreseeing the future.

*   *   *

Next day I was back at Limerick by the middle of the afternoon. Going into the ante-room I found no one there except Kegworthy. It was Sunday, and the others were all out or having a bit of extra sleep.

"There's been an old boy up here asking for you. He said he'd come back again later," said Kegworthy, adding as an afterthought, "Have a drink."

I mention the afterthought because it was a too-frequent utterance of his. Kegworthy was one of the most likeable men at the Depot; there were only two formidable things about him: his physique—he was a magnificent heavy-weight boxer—and his mess bill for drinks. I had seen

several fine men trying to drown the War in whisky, but
never a more good-humoured one than Kegworthy. There
were no half-measures about him, however, and it was
really getting rather serious. Anyhow the mess-waiter
brought him another large one, and I left him to it.

On my way across the barrack square I saw someone
coming through the gateway. He approached me. He was
elderly, stoutish, with a pink face and a small white moustache; he wore a bowler hat and a smart blue overcoat.
His small light blue eyes met mine and he smiled. He looked
an extraordinarily kind old chap, I thought. We stood
there, and after a moment or two he said "Blarnett". Not
knowing what he meant, I remained silent. It sounded like
some sort of Irish interjection. Observing my mystification,
he amplified it slightly: "I'm Blarnett," he remarked
serenely. So I knew that much about him. His name was
Blarnett. But how did he know who I was? But perhaps he
didn't.

I have recorded this little incident in its entirety because
it was typical of him. Mr. Blarnett was a man who assumed
that everyone knew who he was. It seldom occurred to him
that many things in this world need prefatory explanation.
And on this occasion he apparently took it for granted that
the word Blarnett automatically informed me that he had
seen me out hunting, had heard that I was very keen to
come out again, that the hounds were meeting about four
miles away to-morrow, that he had come to offer me a
mount on one of his horses, and that he would call for me
at the Barracks as punctual as the sun. The word Blarnett
was, in fact, a key which unlocked for me the door into the
County Limerick hunting world. All I had to do was to
follow Mr. Blarnett, and the *camaraderie* of the chase made
the rest of it as easy as falling off a log, or falling off one of
Mr. Blarnett's horses (though these seldom "put a foot
wrong", which was just as well for their owner, who rode
by balance and appeared to remain on the top of his horse
through the agency of a continuous miracle, being a re-
markably good bad rider).

He departed, having communicated all that was necessary, and nothing else. His final words were "Mrs. O'Donnell hopes you'll take tea with her after hunting." I said I should be delighted. "A grand woman, Mrs. O'Donnell," he remarked, and toddled away, leaving me to find out for myself who she was and where he lived. No doubt he unconsciously assumed that I knew. And somehow he made one take it all as a matter of course.

Returning to the ante-room I told Kegworthy how "the old boy" had turned out to be a trump card; "And now look here," I added, "I'd already got a hireling for tomorrow, and you've jolly well got to ride it."

My suggestion seemed to cause him momentary annoyance, for he was, I regret to say, in that slightly "sozzled" state when people are apt to be irrationally pugnacious. "But, you bloody bastard, I've never been out hunting in my life. D'you want me to break my bloody neck?"

"Oh, I'm sorry, old chap, I'd no idea you were so nervous about horses."

"What's that? Are *you* telling me I'm nervous? Show me the something Irishman who says that and I'll knock his something head off."

His competitive spirit having been stimulated, it was easy to persuade him that he would enjoy every minute of it, and it was obvious that a day in the country would do him no harm at all. I told him that I'd already hired a wild Irishman with a ramshackle Ford car to take me to the meet, so he could go in that. I assumed that Mr. Blarnett and his horses would call at the Barracks, as he'd said nothing about any other arrangements. So the next morning I was waiting outside the gates in good time. After forty minutes I was still waiting and the situation looked serious when Kegworthy joined me—the Ford car being now just about due to arrive. Shortly afterwards it did arrive, and Mr. Blarnett was in it, wearing a perfectly cut pink hunting coat, with a bunch of violets in his buttonhole. He looked vaguely delighted to see us, but said nothing, so we climbed in, and the car lurched wildly away to the meet, the driver grinning ecstatically round at us when he missed a donkey and cart by inches when swerving round a sharp corner. Mr. Blarnett did not trouble himself to tell us how he came to be sharing Kegworthy's conveyance. With top hat firmly on his head and a white apron over his knees to keep his breeches from getting dirty, he sat there like a child that has been instructed to keep itself clean and tidy until it arrives at the party. And after all, what was there for him to explain? We were being bumped and jolted along a rough road at forty miles an hour, and this obviously implied that the horses had been sent on to the meet. We passed them just before we got there, and Mr. Blarnett revealed their identity by leaning out of the car and shouting "I have me flask" to the groom, who grinned and touched his hat. The flask, which had been brandished as ocular proof, was very large, and looked like a silver-stoppered truncheon.

It was a fine morning and there was quite a large crowd at the cross roads, where the hounds were clustering round the hunt servants on a strip of grass in front of an inn.

Having pulled up with a jerk which nearly shot us out of our seats, we alighted, and Mr. Blarnett, looking rather as if he'd just emerged from a cold dip in the ocean, enquired "Am I acquainted with your officer friend?" A formal introduction followed. "My friend Kegworthy is riding one of Mike Shehan's horses. He's having his first day's hunting," I explained, and then added, "His first day's hunting in Ireland"; hoping thereby to give Kegworthy a fictitious advantage over his total lack of experience.

Mr. Blarnett, in a confidential undertone, now asked, "Will you take something before we start?" Powerless to intervene I followed them to the inn. Mr. Blarnett's popularity became immediately apparent. Everyone greeted him like a long-lost brother, and I also became aware that he was universally known as "The Mister".

They all seemed overjoyed to see The Mister, though most of them had seen him out hunting three days the week before; and The Mister responded to their greetings with his usual smiling detachment. He took it for granted that everybody liked him, and seemed to attribute it to their good nature rather than to his own praiseworthiness.

But was it altogether advisable, I wondered, that he should confer such a large and ill-diluted glass of whisky on such a totally inexperienced man to hounds as Kegworthy? For the moment, however, his only wish seemed to be that the whole world should drink his health. And they did. And would have done so once again had time permitted. But the hounds were about to move off, and The Mister produced his purse with a lordly air, and the landlord kept the change, and we went out to find our horses.

Had I been by myself I should have been sitting on my hireling in a state of subdued excitement and eagerness, scrutinizing the hounds with a pseudo-knowing eye, and observing everyone around me with the detached interest of a visiting stranger. But I was with The Mister, and he made it all feel not quite serious and almost dreamlike. It couldn't have been the modicum of cherry brandy I'd sipped for politeness' sake which made the proceedings seem a sort of extravaganza of good-humoured absurdity.

There was The Mister, solemnly handing his immense flask to the groom, who inserted it in a leather receptacle attached to the saddle. And there was Kegworthy, untying the strings of The Mister's white apron; he looked happy and rather somnolent, with his cap on one side and his crop projecting from one of his trench boots.

Even The Mister's horses seemed in a trance-like condition, although the bustle and fluster of departure was in full swing around them. The Mister having hoisted himself into the saddle, I concentrated on launching Kegworthy into the unforeseeable. I had ridden the hireling before and knew it to be quiet and reliable. But before I had time to offer any advice or assistance, he had mounted heavily, caught the horse by the head, and was bumping full-trot down the road after the rest of the field. His only comment had been: "Tell Mother I died bravely."

"You'll be following to bring him home," said The Mister to our motor-driver, who replied that sure to God it was the grandest hunt we'd be having from the Gorse. We then jogged sedately away.

"Will you be staying long in Limerick?" he asked. I told

him that I might be ordered off to Egypt any day—perhaps to-morrow, perhaps not for a couple of weeks. This seemed to surprise him. "To Egypt? Will you be fighting the Egyptians then?" No, it was the Turks, I told him. "Ah, the Turks, bad luck to them! It crossed me mind when I said it that I had it wrong about the Egyptians."

A quarter of a mile away the tail end of the field could be seen cantering up a green slope to the Gorse. It was a beautiful still morning and the air smelt of the earth.

"'Ark!" exclaimed The Mister, pulling up suddenly. (Dropped aitches were with him a sure sign of cerebral excitement.) From the far side of the covert came a long-drawn view-halloa, which effectively set The Mister in motion. "Go on, boy, go on! Don't be waiting about for me. Holy Mother, you'll be getting no hunting with them Egyptians!" So I went off like a shot out of a gun, leaving him to ride the hunt in his own time. My horse was a grand mover; luckily the hounds turned toward me, and soon I was in the same field with them. Of the next forty minutes I can only say that it was all on grass and the banks weren't too formidable, and the pace just good enough to make it exciting. There was only one short check, and when they had marked their fox to ground I became aware that he had run a big ring and we were quite near the Gorse where we found him. I had forgotten all about Kegworthy, but he now reappeared, perspiring freely and considerably elated. "How did you manage it?" I asked. He assured me that he'd shut his eyes and hung on to the back of the saddle at every bank and the horse had done the rest. The Mister was now in a glow of enthusiasm and quite garrulous. "Sure that mare you're riding is worth five hundred guineas if she's worth a penny bun," he ejaculated, and proceeded to drink the mare's health from that very large flask of his.

*   *   *

As I have already suggested, there was something mysterious about The Mister—a kind of innocence which made people love him and treat him as a perennial joke. But, so far, I knew next to nothing about him, since he took it for granted that one knew everything that he knew; and the numerous hunting people to whom he'd introduced me during a rather dull and uneventful afternoon's sport took everything about The Mister for granted; so on the whole very little definite information about anything had emerged.

"How the hell did he make his money?" asked Kegworthy, as we sat after dinner comparing our impressions of the day's sport and social experience. "Men like The Mister get rid of their money quick enough, but they don't usually make any," he added.

"He certainly gives one the impression of being 'self-made'," I remarked. "Perhaps he won fifty thousand in a sweepstake. But if he'd done that he'd still be telling everyone about it, and would probably have given most of it away by now."

"Perhaps he's in the hands of trustees," suggested Kegworthy. I agreed that it might be so, and nominated Mrs. O'Donnell as one of them. Of Mrs. O'Donnell at any rate, we knew for certain that she had given us a "high-tea" after hunting which had made dining in the mess seem almost unthinkable. It had been a banquet. Cold salmon and snipe and unsurpassable home-made bread and honey had indeed caused us to forget that there was a war on; while as for Mrs. O'D. herself, in five minutes she made me feel that I'd known her all my life and could rely on her assistance in any emergency. It may have been only her Irish exuberance, but it all seemed so natural and homely in that solid plainly-furnished dining-room where everything was for use and comfort more than for ornament.

The house was a large villa, about a mile from the barracks—just outside the town. There I sat, laughing and joking, and puffing my pipe, and feeling fond of the old Mister who had reached an advanced stage of cronydom with Kegworthy, while between them they diminished a decanter of whisky. And then Mrs. O'Donnell asked me whether I played golf; but before I could reply the maid called her out of the room to the telephone, which enabled the word "golf" to transport me from Ireland to Scotland

and see myself cleaning my clubs in my room at the hydro,
and deciding that the only thing to do was to go back to
the War again. How serious that decision had been, and
how blithely life was obliterating it until this visualized
memory evoked by the mention of "golf" had startled me
into awareness of the oddity of my surroundings!

*   *   *

Every day that I went out with the Limerick Hounds
was, presumably, my last; but I was able to make several
farewell appearances, and I felt that each day was something to the good; these were happy times, and while they
lasted I refused to contemplate my Egyptian future. Mentally, I became not unlike The Mister, whose motto—if he
ever formulated anything so definite as a motto—was "we
may all of us be dead next week so let's make the best of
this one". He took all earthly experience as it came and
allowed life to convey him over its obstacles in much the
same way as his horses carried him over the Irish banks.
His vague geniality seemed to embrace the whole human
species. One felt that if Hindenburg arrived in Limerick The
Mister would receive him without one tedious query as to
his credentials. He would merely offer to mount him, and
proudly produce him at the meet next morning. "Let me
introduce me friend Marshal Hindenbird," he would say,
riding serenely up to the Master. And if the Master de-
murred, The Mister would remark, "Be reasonable,
Master. Isn't the world round, and we all on it?"

He was a man who had few forethoughts and no after-
thoughts, and I am afraid that this condition was too often
artificially induced. He and Kegworthy had this in common; they both brimmed over with *bonhomie*, and (during
the period when I knew them) neither could have told me
much about the previous evening. In The Mister's case it
didn't matter much; he was saddled with no responsibilities, and what he felt like next morning was neither
here nor there. He looked surprisingly well on this regime,
and continued to take the world into his confidence. (He
was either solemnly sober or solemnly tipsy; his intermedi-

ate state was chatty, though his intermediate utterances weren't memorable.) But Kegworthy's convivialities were a serious handicap to his efficiency as an officer, though so far it had been "overlooked".

He did not make a second appearance in the saddle. But about a week after his début, when I was getting formal permission from the Assistant-Adjutant to go out hunting the next day, he suggested that I should take Kegworthy with me and get him, to put it candidly, sobered down. The meet was twenty-three miles away, which made it all the better for the purpose. So it was arranged. The Mister was mounting me, and we were to call for him with the erratic Ford car at Mrs. O'Donnell's house (which was where he lived).

It was a pouring wet morning and blowing half a gale. Kegworthy, who said he was feeling like hell, was unwilling to start, but I assured him that the rain would soon blow over. Mrs. O'Donnell came out on to her doorstep, and while we were waiting under the porch for The Mister, she asked me to try and bring him straight home after hunting. "The O'Hallorans are coming to dinner—and of course we are expecting you and Mr. Kegworthy to join us. But Mrs. O'Halloran's a bit stiff and starched; and The Mister's such a terrible one for calling on his friends on the way back; and it isn't barley water they offer him." At this moment The Mister came out, looking very festive in his scarlet coat and canary waistcoat. He was optimistic about the weather and I tried to feel hopeful that I should bring him and Kegworthy home "the worse" for nothing stronger than water.

The maid now appeared carrying The Mister's hat box and flask; he was helped into an enormous overcoat with an astrakhan collar which Mrs. O'Donnell turned up for him so that his countenance was almost completely concealed. He then put on an immense pair of fur gloves, pulled his voluminous tweed cap down over his nose, and gave Mrs. O'Donnell a blandly humorous look which somehow suggested that he knew that whatever he did she couldn't be angry with him. And he was right, for he really was a most likeable man. "Now Mister," she said, "bear it well in your mind that Mrs. O'Halloran and her daughter are dining with us this evening."

"Be easy about that," he replied. "Don't I know that Mrs. O'Halloran is like Limerick itself? Would you think I'm one to overlook the importance of her?" With these words he plunged deliberately under the low hood of the car, settled himself down, and remained silent until we were about half-way to the meet. Kegworthy, hunched up in his corner, showed no sign of expecting his day in the country to be a success. But the driver was getting every ounce out of his engine, through the din of which he occasionally addressed some lively and topically-local comment to The Mister, who nodded philosophically from his astrakhan enclosure. As we proceeded, the road became rough and the surroundings hilly. And the weather, if possible, grew worse.

"What sort of country is it we're going to to-day?" I enquired of the driver.

"Sure it's the wildest place you ever set eyes on. There's rocks and crags where a jackass could get to ground and sleep easy," he replied, adding, "I'm thinking, Mr. Blarnett, that the dogs'll do better to stay at home on such a day as this."

The Mister opened one eye and remarked that it would sure be madness to go up on the hills in such weather. "But me friend Tom Philipson will give us a bite to eat," he added serenely, "and you'll travel far before you find the like of the old brandy that he'll put in your glass." He nudged Kegworthy with his elbow, and I inwardly hoped that Tom Philipson's hospitality wouldn't be too alcoholic.

For it was my solemn purpose that we should travel away from brandy rather than that it should be an object of pilgrimage. Tom Philipson, it transpired, was the owner of a big house; he also owned some of the surrounding country, the aspect of which fully justified its reputation for roughness and infertility. The village which was part of his property appeared to be an assortment of stone hovels in very bad repair.

I may as well say at once that when we arrived at Tom Philipson's the M.F.H. had already decided that hunting was out of the question, and was about to go home. The hounds had already departed. Hospitality was all that awaited us, and after all there was nothing wrong with an early luncheon in a spacious and remote old Irish mansion. There was nothing wrong with Tom Philipson either. He was middle-aged, a famous character in that part of the world, and had something of the grand manner about him. My recollection of him is that he was extremely good company, and full of rich-flavoured Irish talk. What could have been more delightful than to sit in a dignified dining-room and listen to such a man, while the rain pelted against the windows and a wood fire glowed and blazed in the immense fireplace, and the fine old burnished silver shone reflectively on the mahogany table? I can imagine myself returning to the barracks after such an experience, my visit having been prolonged late into the afternoon while Tom Philipson showed me the treasures of his house. What charm it all had, ruminates my imagined self, remembering that evocative portrait of Tom Philipson's grandmother by Sir Thomas Lawrence, and the stories he'd told me about the conquests she made in Dublin and afterwards in London. Yes, I imagine myself soaking it all up and taking it all home with me to digest, rejoicing in my good fortune at having acquired such a pleasant period-example of an Irish country mansion, where one's host reticently enjoyed showing his heirlooms to an appreciative visitor. I should remember a series of dignified seldom-used rooms smelling of the past; and a creaking uneven passage with a window-seat at the end of it and a view of the wild green park beyond straggling spiral yews, and the evening clouds lit with the purplish bloom of rainy weather.

And then a door would be opened for me with a casual, "I'm not a great reader, but the backs of old books are companionable things for a man who sits alone in the evenings"—and there would be—an unravished eighteenth and early nineteenth-century library, where obsolete Sermons and Travels in mellow leather bindings might be neighboured by uncut copies of the first issues of Swift and Goldsmith, and Jane Austen might be standing demurely on a top shelf in her original boards. And Tom Philipson would listen politely while one explained that his first editions of Smollett's novels were really in positively mint condition. . . .

But this is all such stuff as dreams are made of. What authentically happened was that we had a hell of a good lunch and Tom Philipson told some devilish good stories, and The Mister was enchanted, and Kegworthy enjoyed every minute of it, and both of them imbibed large quantities of Madeira, Moselle, port wine and brandy and became very red in the face in consequence. This made me feel uneasy, especially as they seemed quite likely to sit there all the afternoon; the fact remained that at half-past three Kegworthy was lighting his second large cigar and Tom Philipson was pressing him to try some remarkable old Jamaica rum, though neither he nor the now semi-intoxicated Mister needed any "pressing" at all. I felt a bit hazy in the head myself.

Our host, however, was a man who knew how to handle an inconclusive situation. His manner stiffened perceptibly when Kegworthy showed signs of becoming argumentative about Irish politics and also addressed him as "old bean". Daylight was diminishing through the tall windows and Tom Philipson strolled across to observe that the bad weather had abated, adding that our drive back to Limerick was a long one. This hint would have been lost on my companions, so I clinched it by asking for our motor. In the entrance hall, which bristled with the horned heads of sporting trophies, The Mister gazed wonderingly around him while he was being invested with his overcoat. "Mother of God, it must have been a grand spectacle, Tom, when you were pursuing the wild antelope across the prairie with your gun," he remarked, putting up a gloved hand to stroke the nose of a colossal elk. We then said grateful good-byes to the elk's owner, and our homeward journey was begun.

.I say "begun", because it wasn't merely a matter of being bundled through the gloom until we arrived at Mrs. O'Donnell's door. About half-way home, The Mister—who had said nothing since his tribute to Tom Philipson's glory as a gunman—suddenly said to the driver, "Stop at O'Grady's."

Soon afterwards we drew up, and The Mister led the way into a comfortless little house, where Mr. O'Grady made us welcome in a bleak front room, glaringly lit by a lamp which caused a strong smell of paraffin oil to be the keynote of the atmospheric conditions. There seemed no special reason why we were calling on O'Grady, but he handed each of us a tumbler containing three parts raw whisky to one part water. While I was wondering how on earth I could dispose of mine without drinking it, my companions swallowed the fiery fluid unblenchingly, and did not say "No" to a second dose. O'Grady sustained the conversation with comments on what the hounds had been doing lately and what the foxes had been doing to his poultry. The Mister blinked at the lamp and made noises which somewhat suggested a meditative hen. When we got up to go, he remarked in confidential tones to O'Grady, "I have yet to make up me mind about the little red horse that ye desire to sell me." This, apparently, epitomized the object of our visit to O'Grady. My head ached, but the night air was refreshing, though I had some doubts as to its effect on my obviously "half-seas-over" friends. Hope died in me when The Mister, after getting into the car, instructed the driver to "stop at Finnigan's".

I did not ask The Mister why he wanted to stop at Finnigan's, nor did I ask him not to. At the best of times he wasn't a man whose wishes one felt inclined to frustrate, and he was now alcoholically impervious to suggestion. He had it in mind that he wanted to stop at Finnigan's, and he had nothing else in mind, one concluded. The only information he volunteered was that Finnigan was an old friend of his. "I knew him when I had but one coat to my back." It would have been useless to remind him that his dinner-coat awaited him at Mrs. O'Donnell's, and that his heavily-enveloped form had been by no means steady on its legs when he emerged from O'Grady's. There was nothing now that I could do except assist him out of the car and steer him through Finnigan's front door, which was open to all-comers, since it was neither more nor less than a village pub. In the bar-parlour about a dozen Irish characters were increasing the sale of malted spirits and jabbering with vehement voices. They welcomed The Mister like one of themselves, and his vague wave of a fur-gloved hand sufficed to signify "whiskies all round" and a subsequent drinking of The Mister's health. "Long life to ye, Mister Blarnett," they chorused, and The Mister's reply was majestic. "Long life to ye all, and may I never in me grandeur forget that I was born no better than any one of you and me money made in America." His voice was husky, but the huskiness was not induced by emotion. The air was thick with bad tobacco smoke and I was longing to be back in Limerick, but there was something very touching in the sight of the tipsy old Mister. There he sat in his scarlet coat, nodding his white head and beaming hazily around him, every bit as glad to be among these humble people as he had been in Tom Philipson's fine house. More at home, perhaps, in his heart of hearts, and dimly aware of his youth and those hard times before he went to the States and—Heaven knows how—made, and failed to be swindled out of—his fortune. Kegworthy and I were completely out of the picture (I, because I felt shy, and Kegworthy because he was in a condition verging on stupor). Meanwhile Finnigan, elderly and foxy-faced, leant his elbows on the bar and held forth about the troubled state of the country. "There'll be houses burnt and lives lost before the year's ended," he said, "and you officers, friends of Mr. Blarnett's though you be, had better be out of Ireland than in it, if you set value on your skins." A gruff murmur greeted this utterance, and I took a sip of my whisky, which half-choked me and tasted strong of smoke. But The Mister remained seraphically unperturbed. He rose unsteadily, was helped into his overcoat, and then muttered the following valediction: "I'd be remaining among you a while longer, boys, but there's company expected at Mrs. O'Donnell's, and it's my tuxedo I'll be wearing to-night and the pearl studs to my shirt." Swaying slightly, he seemed to be collecting his thoughts for a final effort of speech; having done so, he delivered the following cryptic axiom: "In politics and religion, be pleasant to both sides. Sure, we'll all be dead drunk on the Day of Judgment." Table-thumpings and other sounds of approval accompanied him as he staggered to the door, having previously emptied all his loose silver into the hand of his old friend Finnigan. During the last stage of the journey he was warblesome, singing to himself in a tenor crooning that seemed to come from a long way off. I entered Mrs. O'Donnell's door with one of them on each arm.

Explanations were unnecessary when she met us in the hall. A single glance showed her how the day's hunting had ended. I had brought them back, and they were both of them blind to the world.

This was unfortunate, and should have precluded their presence at the dinner-table. But Mrs. O'Donnell had already got herself into a dark green bespangled evening dress and was deciding to be undaunted. I was about to suggest that I should take Kegworthy straight home, when she drew me aside and said in an urgent undertone, "They've three-quarters of an hour in which to recover themselves. For the love of God make Kegworthy put his head in cold water, and I'll be getting The Mister up to his room." Her large and competent presence created optimism, so I carried out her instructions and then deposited Kegworthy in the drawing-room. His manner was now muzzily morose, and I couldn't feel any confidence in him as a social asset. Mrs. O'Donnell bustled back, and she and I kept up appearances gallantly until Mrs. O'Halloran and her daughter were announced. Mrs. O'Halloran was what one might call a semi-dowager; the first impression she made on me was one of almost frumpishly constrained dignity, and the impression remained unaltered throughout the evening. She moved in an aura of unhurrying chaperonage and one felt disapproval in the background of her mind. She began by looking very hard at my field boots, whereupon Mrs. O'Donnell enlivened the situation with a fluent and even florid account of the day's adventures.

"Miles and miles they went in the wild weather, and the hounds not able to hunt—God be praised for that, for my heart was in my mouth when I thought of The Mister destroying himself over those bogs and boulders on the Mullagharier Mountains. And then what must Clancy's car do but break down twice on the way home and they five miles from anywhere." Mrs. O'Halloran signified her acceptance of the story by a stiff inclination of her head, which was surmounted by two large lacquered combs and an abbreviated plume dyed purple. She herself seemed to have travelled many miles that evening—from the end of the eighteenth century perhaps—drawn over rough roads at a footpace in some lumbering, rumbling family coach. This notion had just crossed my mind when The Mister made his appearance, which was impeccable except for the fact that he was carrying in one hand a glass of something which I assumed to be whisky.

By some Misterish miracle he had recovered his equilibrium—or leguilibrium—and was quite the grand seigneur in his deportment. His only social disadvantage was that he seemed incapable of articulate utterance. Whenever a remark was made he merely nodded like a mandarin. Kegworthy also was completely uncommunicative, but looked less amiable. We followed the ladies into the dining-room, and thus began a dinner which largely consisted of awful silences. At one end of the table sat The Mister; Mrs. O'Halloran was to the right of him and Miss O'Halloran was to the left of him. Next to Miss O'Halloran sat me; Mrs. O'Donnell, of course, faced The Mister, so Kegworthy's position may be conjectured. He was, beyond all conjecture, sitting beside Mrs. O'Halloran.

Mrs. O'Donnell and I did all the work. Kegworthy being a non-starter, she talked across him to Mrs. O'Halloran, while I made heavy weather with Miss O'Halloran, who relied mainly on a nervous titter, while her mamma relied entirely on monosyllabic decorum. As the meal went on I became seriously handicapped by the fact that I got what is known as "the giggles". Every time I looked across at Mrs. O'Halloran her heavily powdered face set me off again, and I rather think that Mrs. O'Donnell became similarly affected. The Mister only addressed two remarks to Mrs. O'Halloran. The first one referred to the European war. "Tom Philipson was telling me to-day that we should be putting more pressure on Prussia." Mrs. O'Halloran glacially agreed, but it led to nothing further, as her attention was distracted by Kegworthy, who, in attacking a slab of stiff claret jelly, shot a large piece off his plate, chased it with his spoon, and finally put it in his mouth with his fingers. This gave me an excuse to laugh aloud, but Mrs. O'Halloran didn't even smile. When the port had been round once The Mister raised his glass and said, with a vague air of something special being expected of him. "If there's one man in Limerick I esteem, sure to God it's your husband. Long life to Mr. O'Halloran." At this, Kegworthy, who had been looking more morose than ever, made his only audible contribution to the festive occasion.

"Who the hell's O'Halloran?" he enquired. His intonation implied hostility. There was, naturally enough, a ghastly pause in the proceedings. Then Mrs. O'Donnell arose and ushered her guests out of the room in good order.

There I sat, and for a long time neither of my companions moved. Closing my eyes, I thought about that dinner-party, and came to the conclusion that it had been funny.

When I opened them again I ascertained that both The Mister and Kegworthy were fast asleep. Nothing more remains to be told, except that soon afterwards I took Kegworthy home and put him to bed.

*   *   *

On my last day in Ireland I went out in soft sunshiny weather for a final half-day with the hounds. The meet was twelve miles off and I'd got to catch the 4.30 train to Dublin, so I had to keep a sharp eye on my watch. The Mister was mournful about my departure, and anathematized the Egyptians wholeheartedly, for he couldn't get rid of his notion that it was they who were requiring my services as a soldier. I felt a bit mournful myself as my eyes took in the country with its distant villages and gleams of water, its green fields and white cottages, and the hazy transparent hills on the horizon—sometimes silver-grey and sometimes that deep azure which I'd seen nowhere but in Ireland.

We had a scrambling hunt over a rough country, and I had all the fun I could find, but every stone wall I jumped felt like good-bye for ever to "this happy breed of men, this little world", in other words the Limerick Hunt, which had restored my faith in my capacity to be heedlessly happy. How kind they were, those friendly fox-hunters, and how I hated leaving them.

At half-past two The Mister and I began to look for Clancy's car, which contained his groom and was to take us home. But the car was on the wrong side of a big covert, and while we were following it, it was following us. Much flustered, we at last succeeded in encountering it, and Clancy drove us back to Mrs. O'Donnell's in a wild enthusiastic spurt.

Mrs. O'Donnell had a woodcock ready for my tea, and I consumed it in record time. Then there was a mad rush to the station, where my baggage was awaiting me, plus a group of Fusilier friends. The Assistant-Adjutant was at his post, assuring the engine driver that he must on no account start without me, mail-train or no mail-train. With thirty seconds to spare I achieved my undesirable object, and the next thing I knew was that I was leaning out of the carriage window and waving good-bye to them all—waving good-bye to warm-hearted Mrs. O'Donnell— waving good-bye to the dear old Mister.

PART THREE: SHERSTON'S DIARY:
FOUR MONTHS

I

Wednesday, February 13th. Left Southampton on Monday evening and got to Cherbourg by 2 a.m. Stayed last night at Rest Camp about three miles out, close to large château, used as Red Cross hospital. It is a mild grey morning, with thrushes singing like spring. I am a little way from the camp, sitting on a bundle of brushwood under a hedge. The country round, with its woods of pine, oak, and beech, and its thorn and hazel hedges, might be anywhere in the home counties—Surrey for preference.

I came up on deck on the *Antrim* on Tuesday morning at 6.30, and found we were in Cherbourg harbour.

It was just before dawn—everything asleep and strange, with lights burning round the harbour and on shore. Slowly the dark water became steel-grey and the clouded sky whitened, and the foreign hills and houses emerged from obscurity. All the while the ship hissed and steamed and the wind hummed in the rigging. This is the third time in three years that I've been in France on February 13th. A magpie is scolding among the beeches, and the wind (south-west) bustles among the bare twigs. I have just recaptured that rather pleasant feeling of detachment from all worldly business which comes when one is "back at the War". Nothing much to worry and distract one except the usual boredoms and irritations of "being mucked about" by the army.

To-day we start our 1446-mile train journey to Taranto. It takes more than a week. My companions are Hooper, Howell and Marshall. Camp-commandant (promoted from sergeant-major to major?) asked us: "Anythink else you officers may wish to partake of? . . ."

Have just picked a primrose. Wonder when I shall see another.

February 14th. 6.30 p.m. Have been twenty-seven hours in the train. Not much room to move in our compartment, what with kit and boxes for provisions, which we use as tables and put our candles on. Marshall, very good at finding out things beforehand, bought primus stoves, café-au-lait, and all sorts of useful things at Cherbourg. M. is the best of the three. About 21: big and capable; pockets usually bulging; hopes to be a doctor. Sort of chap who never grumbles—always willing to be helpful. I read most of the time, and they play cards continuously. . . . "Twist; stick", etc. . . . Halt at Bourges to draw rations. Have been reading Pater on Leonardo da Vinci! Funny mixture of crude reality and inward experience. Feel much more free to study other people than last time I was doing this sort of thing. More detached and selfless, somehow. But perhaps it's only because I don't play "Nap" and have been reading Pater—"this sense of the splendour of our experience and its awful brevity".

February 15th. Awoke to find a bright frosty morning and the train in a station for an hour's halt. Crawled on to St. Germain (15 kilos from Lyons). Got there at 12.30 after going through fine country, fir-wooded hills and charming little valleys threaded by shallow rivers. Saw some oxen hauling a tree and a boy standing looking down at the train. The sun shone gloriously and warmed my face as I craned from the window to take in as much of this new part of France as I could. We stay at a rest camp near the station. Bath and lunch and then I went marketing with Marshall. The blue Saône or Rhône—don't know which it is—flowing nobly along. We leave again to-night. Am writing this in Y.M.C.A. hut after dinner. Entertainment going on. Jock sergeant reciting poem by R. W. Service; nervous lance-corporal sang "The truth or a lie, which shall it be?" in a weak voice without any emphasis.

February 17th. 1.30 p.m. Train crawling toward Italian frontier. Bright sun and cold wind. Hard frost last two nights. Feeling ill with fever and chill on insides. Left St.

Germain 2 a.m. yesterday. Bitterly cold in the train. Went through Avignon, Cannes, Nice, etc., and along by the sea in late afternoon. A gaudy parched-looking tourist region. Flowers thrown to the troops and general atmosphere of Cook's tour. Groups of black soldiers in red fez and blue uniform seen at street-ends in brassy sunshine. Beyond Nice the sea looked less "popular", softly crashing on the brimming rocks in the dusk, and I heard it at times during the night, half-sleeping on the seat with my feet somewhere near Marshall's face. Daylight, red and frosty, found us beyond Genoa after much rumbling and clanking through short tunnels in the dark.

February 18th. (Monday morning.) Through Novi and Vochera, where we halt for lunch. Funny way of seeing Italy for the first time, but better than nothing, and inexpensive. Glaring sunlight and cold wind. All the afternoon we crawl through vinelands, with low, blue, delicate-edged hills a few miles away till the sun goes down and leaves an amethyst glow on the horizon, and at 7.30 we reach Bologna.

Jolly companionship of the journey, in spite of animal squalor and so on. Hooper rather hipped and fussy—bad campaigner I fear. Youthful charm and good looks but absence of guts. Howell sensible and philosophic. Was a schoolmaster and played football for Wales. Marshall an absolute marvel, with his jolly face and simple jokes. Tells Hooper to come off his perch and put the kettle on, which isn't well received by the golden-haired one.

February 19th. After a night journey of freezing gloom, the train stopping occasionally at cavernous stations and my insides still behaving atrociously, we reached Faenza about 3 a.m. Turned out at 8 to a sunlit morning and soon found ourselves washing and drinking coffee in a hotel, moderately comfortable. Tall clean narrow streets; market place full of gossip and babble of cloaked and hooded unshaven middle-aged men, with a sprinkling of soldiers in grey with yellow collars. The fountain was festooned with ice, like melted lead.

February 20th. Left Faenza 9 p.m. and began the journey

along the Adriatic coast. Cold morning; snow lying thin and half-melting; grey sky. On our right the low hills streaked with white. On the left (how accurate I am) the flat lavender sea, flecked and broken with foam, and the slate-coloured horizon. Breakfast at Castellamarie.

Foggia about 11 p.m. Still very cold.

February 21st. Awoke in twilight to find we were going through olive orchards (hoary ancients bent and twisted), with rough stone walls. First time I've seen olive trees. Then the sun came up and dazzled me through almond blossom, with delicate glimpses of the Adriatic a mile or two away. Quite idyllic.

About noon, we come to Brindisi (about which I know nothing except Edward Lear's limerick), and I take a shower bath and dry myself in the sun and a bracing breeze, in a garden near the railway where "ablution-sheds", etc. are put up among fig trees, vine-pergola, and almond trees, with a group of umbrella pines at one end shadowing an old stone seat for summer afternoons. Felt like staying there.

On again about 3—the final stage to Taranto—crossing a flat cultivated plain fringed and dotted with tufts and cloudy haze of pink and white blossom, with green of prickly pears(?) and young corn, the wind swaying the dull silver of tossing olive trees—all in the glare of spring sunshine. Bare fig trees are the most naked trees I've ever seen.

At sunset we passed Grottaglie, a town on a hill; flat-roofed white houses, one above another, and an old brown castle with a tower and sheer wall at the top of it all. Orchards in bloom below, already invaded by shadow. The town faced west, and seemed lit from within, smouldering and transparent and luminous like a fire-opal. It looked like a dream city. (Probably a damned smelly place for all that.) Arrived Taranto about 9, in moonlight.

Friday, February 22nd, 6 p.m. In a tent; rest camp. Walked along the harbour after lunch in glaring sunshine and shrewd wind. Blue water; rusty parched hills away on the other side. Towns far away like heaps of white stones. Glad of my good field-glasses, I sat on a rock and listened to the slapping gurgle of the water (clear as glass), while the other three straddled along the path, swinging their sticks and looking rather out of place without a pier. This journey will always come back to me when I think of an absurd song which everyone sings, hums, whistles, and shouts incessantly. "Good-bye-ee; don't cry-ee; wipe the tear, baby dear, from your eye-ee," etc. There is something a bit grown-up-babyish about Marshall's good-humoured face; the song suits him somehow!

Slept in the train again last night—alongside the station platform—and had my watch stolen. (I'd put it on my box-table near the window, so the thief had only to put his hand in.) Luckily my fire-opal was round my neck, but losing one's watch is pretty serious. All sorts of officers here —many on their way home on leave. Not many intelligent sensitive faces. (The doctors look different from the others, mostly with wise, kind faces.) The usual crowd playing poker in the mess all the time. Staff-officers, colonels, majors, Australians, flying-men—all sorts—their eyes meet one's own for a moment and then slide down to look for a medal-ribbon.

After dinner I came out into the chilly moonlight; the moonlight-coloured bell-tents had tracery of shadows on them from the poor old olive trees that are left high and dry in this upstart camp, like wise old men being mobbed. Someone was strumming on a piano in the concert marquee behind our tent-lines. I lifted a flap and peered into fantastic dimness where a few lights made a zany-show of leaping shadows and swaying whiteness. On the stage (looked at from behind) a group was rehearsing. A big man was doing a bit of gag before stepping back two paces to begin his song. "Give 'em a bit of Fred Emney!" someone shouted. Then a small man jumped into the light and did some posturing—chin out and curved Hebrew beak coming down to a thin-lipped mouth.

Another little Jew whispered to me (I was now inside the tent) "That's Sid Whelan—the other's his brother Albert" —evidently expecting me to be thrilled. They must have

been well-known comedians. (All of them belong to the
Jewish Battalion, which is awaiting embarkation here.)

Rumour in the mess to-night that "Jericho has fallen".

February 24th. Am now on board the P. and O. boat
Kashgar. Lying in my bunk alone with Conrad's *Chance* and
feeling all the better for being comfortable. Across the
cabin steals a patch of dusty evening sunshine. Feet pace
the deck above; cabin doors slam down below. The swish
of the sea and the drone of a gusty breeze; and me in the
middle of the longest journey of my life. Boat still in harbour.

February 26th. 7 a.m. Feeling much better this morning
after headache and feverishness since Sunday night. Boat
got under way yesterday afternoon and has since been
ploughing the smooth Mediterranean—very well-behaved
voyage so far. When going on deck for boat-drill, officers
sing "Nearer my God to Thee". Can't say I've observed
anything interesting so far. The sea is rather like a Royal
Academy picture and the officer-conversations dull beyond
description. I don't feel much sympathy for them. (I've
felt pretty rotten, though, since Sunday.) But they seem so
self-satisfied, with their card-playing and singing "Chu-
Chin-Chow", etc. Outside the saloon door one passes from
cheap cigarette smoke to what Conrad calls "the brilliant
evidence of the awful loneliness of the hopeless obscure in-
significance of our globe lost in the splendid revelation of a
glittering soulless universe". (A bit over-written surely!
Must avoid that sort of thing myself.)

The Gulf of Taranto was a level steel-blue plain. Low on
the horizon, the mountainous coast was like a soft rain-
cloud on the sea—a ragged receding line of hills extending
to dim capes and shoals which merged themselves in the
hazy romance of sunset. This was the last I saw of Italy. On
the other side of the ship it was already night, with a full
moon dancing on the waves.

That was written by me (not Conrad) on Monday evening. But I really must try not to be so bloody serious.

February 27. Weather fine. Brain refuses to work. Still
feeling rather seedy.

February 28. Arrived Alexandria after exactly three days' voyage.

A clear, gentle-coloured afternoon; blue sea; creamy, brick-red, terra-cotta, and grey city; wharves and docks with drifting smoke and thickets of masts and funnels. Sunshine, not glaring. Everything breezy, cheerful, and busy.

British officers watch it all for a while, nonchalantly— then go below for tea. I also; no more excited than the rest of them. . . .

Shall I find anything tremendous and heroic out here, I wonder? Troops in a warm-climate sideshow. Urbane, compared with France. Rather the same sort of thing as this dock with its glassy dark water and mild night air; stars, gold moon, dark ships, quiet lights, and sound of soldiers singing—safe in port once more.

March 2. Left Alexandria 10.30 last night. Arrived Base Camp, Kantara, 10 this morning. Bought a watch in Alexandria. It is hexagonal and was very expensive. If anything like the face of the dago who sold it to me, it will let me down badly as regards time-keeping.

Same day. (No. 1 Base Depot.) Lying in tent. Valise spread on sand. Glare of sunshine outside. Splitting headache (inside).

Sounds. Thrumming of piano in officers' mess—not quite out of earshot.

Lorries rumbling along road fifty yards away. Troops marching and whistling. Bagpipes—a long way off. (So is Scotland.) Egyptian labourers go past, singing a monotonous chorus, which seems to go up into the light, somehow.

Officers' Mess; analysis. Drinks; drinks. Writing some letters. Someone says "Only one mail in the last three weeks." Bored men reading stale *Bystanders* and other illustrated papers. Amy Woodforde Finden's oriental popularities being pot-pourri'd on the tin-kettle piano. Otherwise anteroom quite cool and pleasant. Slim grey birds chirping in the roof. Onions for lunch. Why put that down, I wonder? . . . Wounded officer back from hospital said to me "They bung you back quick enough nowadays. I can hardly walk!"

This morning. Suez Canal from train. Garden at Ismalia

—a bit of blossom and greenery among sandy wastes. Waiting at Canal bridge for two big ships to go by. Talked to two Irish officers in the train. One knew Ledwidge the poet, and said "he could imitate birds and call them to him"—a tiny glimpse of "real life" in this desert of officer mentality. Am feeling ill and keep on coughing.

March 4. Marshall and I posted to 25th Battalion to-day. Moved across to Yeomanry Base Camp (half a minute's walk!). Another day of arid sunshine and utter blankness. The sand and the tents and the faces—all seem meaningless. Just a crowd of people killing time. Time wasted in waste places. People go up to the Line almost gladly, feeling that there's some purpose in life after all. Those who remain here scheme to get leave; and having got it, go aimlessly off to Cairo, Port Said or Ismalia, to spend their money on eating and drinking and being bored. One hears a certain amount of "war-shop" being talked, but it hasn't the haggard intensity of Western Front war-shop. The whole place has the empty clearness of a moving-picture. Movements of men and munitions against a background of soulless drought. The scene is drawn with unlovely distinctness. Every living soul is here against his will. And when the War ends the whole thing will vanish and the sand will blot out all traces of the men who came here.

Along the main road that runs through the camp, parties of Turkish prisoners march, straggling and hopeless— slaves of war, guarded by a few British soldiers with fixed bayonets. They too are killing time. One of them was shot last week, for striking an officer.

March 8. Went to Port Said for the day with Marshall. A dreary place; but it takes more than Port Said to depress M. Bought Tolstoy's *War and Peace* and Scott's *Antiquary.* ("Everyman" editions were all they had.) Funny books to buy at Port Said of all places in the world. Seems funny to me, anyhow. Sort of thing that would amuse Rivers.

Watching sunset waves foaming and coming in rather grandly with a breeze blowing across from Asia Minor (rather nice idea, that), I thought of Rivers—I don't quite know why.

Thinking of him always helps. . . . Port Said also provided me with a dozen wire pipe-cleaners at a penny each. Marshall quite indignant at such profiteering. "No one here except swindlers" he said.

March 10. Left Kantara yesterday evening. Thirteen officers in a cattle truck. Got to Gaza after being bumped and rattled for twelve hours.

March 11. Reached Railhead (Ludd) at 2.30 p.m. Olive trees and almond orchards. Fine hills inland, not unlike Scotland. Last night we went through flat sandy places. About daybreak the country began to be green. Tents among crops and trees all the way up from Gaza. Weather warm and pleasant, with clouds. Thousands of camels in one camp. A few Old Testament pictures of people and villages. Inhabitants seem to live by selling enormous oranges to the troops on the train.

March 12. Just off to Jerusalem, after sleeping in tent at rest camp about a mile from Ludd Station. Self and M. dined in Canteen tent. Talked to Mountain-Battery Major who'd ridden down from Bethlehem. "Don't go to the Garden of Gethsemane," he said. "It's the duddest show I've ever seen!"

First night in Palestine quite pleasant, anyhow. Looked out last thing at calm stars and clouds and quiet candle-glow of bell-tents among olive trees. Large black-headed tits among cactuses. Also a sort of small rook (made same noise as a rook, anyway). Rain in the night. Then sunshine and larks singing. Soft warm air, like English summer. Early this morning, rumble of gun-fire miles away, for about ten minutes. Nothing grim about this Front so far. France was grim, even at Rouen.

Same day. Ramallah. Started at 9.30. (Twelve officers and baggage in a lorry.) Reached 74th Division H.Q. at 4.30. The road climbed and twisted among the hills, which are wild and desolate, strewn with rocks and stones like thousands of sheep. Tractors going up with six-inch howitzers. Ambulances coming down. Leaving Ludd we passed a long procession of grey donkeys loaded with blankets for the troops. At the first halt (Latron, at the foot of the hills) I munched my food in a ruined garden by a stream; frogs croaking and strange notes of birds; wild flowers out.

About 2.30 we entered Jerusalem. Not a very holy looking place. Went straight through into another region of desolate looking hills. Marshall remarked that he wished he'd brought his ruddy Bible with him now. Ramallah is 8 miles north of Jerusalem, on the top of a hill. Taken by us two months ago. Divisional H.Q. a large house with a line of cypresses. Weather cold, grey, and rainy. Yellow flaring sunset. Hills faint purple. Strange medley of soldiers and inhabitants in the narrow village street at dusk. Some of the Hebrews very handsome. Lonely glens and ravines all around, sad and silent, and the hilltops hoary in the twilight. No sound of artillery. In the muddy road I stopped and talked to a man I hadn't seen since I was in the Yeomanry, now a sergeant attached to Divn. H.Q. When I last saw him we were both privates, and in the same troop. That was nearly three and a half years ago, and seems a longish time. They have been made into Infantry, like the battalion I am joining.

March 13. Very wet morning. Our little tent became flooded and miserable, so I went out. Sat in a tent for nearly an hour talking to a private (Middlesex Regiment) while it rained. Told me he'd been twelve years in America with a circus, training trick horses. Gave a gloomy account of the Line here. Very bad country for troops, great hardships, and not much to eat! About noon the sun came out and I walked away from the village. With the better weather the country showed itself as much nicer than it had looked from a distance. Along the stony terraces there are innumerable wild flowers. Red anemones, cyclamen, and others I don't know the names of. Went back along a glen with a cheerful stream, small but companionable. Birds came down there to drink. Sitting on a stone I watched 2 men and 2 women (Arabs) driving some small black and white cattle and two donkeys along the other side of the stream. The cattle turned and looked at me and their owners shouted greetings. I waved back and shouted "Cheeroh!" The cattle-bells sounded just right. Back in the vil-

lage, lorries, limbers, camel-columns, etc. coming and going, and the same old business grinding on. But I felt as if
I'd escaped it all for a few hours.

March 14. Marshall and I walked up to Divisional Sup-
ply Depot, about six miles. Then on to 25th Battalion, another three miles through the usual wild hills where the
Division have been advancing lately. Fine day. Got there
about four o'clock. They are bivouacked on a hillside,
along rocky terraces. The Colonel greeted us genially. He
is a real live lord. (Something to live up to!) I must now
pull myself together and try to be a keen young officer.
Colonel evidently thinks me efficient, owing to my M.C.
and service in France. Am second in command of "C"
Company. Only one other officer. (Company commander
in England on leave.)

March 15. Out from 9 till 4, with the Company, working
at roadmending. Got very wet. Before we started the Brigadier addressed the Battalion; he stood on the terrace above
us, leaning on a five-foot pole. He praised the men for their
recent exploits in chasing "Johnny Turk" over the hills
and ended by saying that he hoped our efforts would soon
get him a Division. The latter remark did him no good at all.

March 17. Heavy rain the last two days. Am sitting in
this canvas shelter with my one candle. Men's voices sing
and talk gruffly in the bivouacs below. Some are singing
hymns. (It is Sunday evening.) Two (B Company) officers
here. One an Oxford man (Magdalen); about 25; gentle
and diffident; reads good books; not a strong character; I
imagine him repeating Kipling's poem "If" to himself and
hoping to be a better man for it. The other is an ex-com-
mercial traveller from Welshpool; aged 35, with a broken
nose and a slight stammer. A considerable character; very
garrulous and amusing.

March 23. Battalion moved 3 miles down the Nablus road
to new camp (on terraces among fig trees). Hot day. Thousands of small purple iris out.

March 26. Seem to be getting on all right. Very easy life,
mending roads.

The Battalion Doctor has made all the difference to me

lately (mentally). Different species from the other officers.
Lean, grimy and brown, he goes grubbing up roots on the
hills; knows every bird; rather like a bird himself. Before
the war used to cruise about on rivers and canals and remote streams studying wild life. Eyes like brown pools;
scrubby moustache; foul pipe; voice somehow suggests
brown water flowing. Feels kind about animals (instead of
shooting them).

Am learning about birds from him. Went out yesterday
and was shown Critchmar's Bunting, Nubian Shrike,
Syrian Jay, Lesser Whitethroat, Redstart, Arabian Wheat-
ear, Goldfinch, and Blackcap. Also a Kestrel and some
Egyptian Vultures. Can't think what I should do without
the Doctor!

March 28. Late afternoon. Quiet and warm. Frogs croaking
in the wet ground up the wadi. Small thorn trees make
clumps of young green up the terraces. At the end of the
wadi there is a water spring; small rills sing their way down
among the stones and over slabs of rock. Pippits and wheat-
ears flit and chirp among the bushes, perch on rocks, or are
busy in the olive branches. On my way home from a walk,
a gazelle got up and fled uphill among the boulders; stood
quite still about 500 yards away, watching me. Then trotted
quietly away. A free creature.

Evening. Warm dusk. The hills looming dark and solemn
all around. Here and there a single dark tree on the skyline.
The moon comes up hazy and clouded with silver-grey
drifts A warm wind blows across the darkening heights.
Below me, the camp is a shrouded glitter of tiny lights scattered on the dusk. Sounds of voices and rattling wheels
which come far-off and clear, small sounds of life in the
vast silence of the night and the hills. Then an eerie yelp-
ing, suddenly breaking off again. Must have been jackals.

I look down on the dim olive-trees where the terraces
wind and climb—wild labyrinthine gardens. Huge head-
stones, slabs, and crags glimmer anciently in the clouded
moonlight, like the tombs of giants, heaved and tilted side-
ways. Some are like enormous well-heads; others are cleft
and piled to form narrow caves. Ghosts might inhabit

them. But they are older than men, older than wars. They are as man first found them. Now they are ramparts of rock tufted with flowers, tangled with clematis and honeysuckle and briar. Thus I describe my sense of peace and freedom. And as I finish writing, someone comes excitedly into the tent with the latest news from France.

The bulletins are getting steadily worse. Names which mean nothing to the others make me aware that the Germans have recaptured all the ground gained in the Somme battles.

March 31. (Easter Sunday.) Out all the afternoon with the Doc. Rain came on and blotted the landscape. (We were on a hill from which the Mountains of Moab are visible on a clear day—rather like a herd of elephants, they look.)

In a ruined tower in a vineyard we smoked our pipes by a blazing fire of dry olive branches. He makes most of the other officers seem purblind, mentally. Says very little about them, and regards them with tolerant and good-humoured detachment. He spotted at once what a good chap Marshall is; but Marshall is being transferred to another Battalion with which he has some previous connection. He will probably be happier there; but I shall miss him.

When I'm alone in the tent I feel a bit heavy-hearted about the news from France, which gets more ominous every day though no one else seems to be worrying much. I read *War and Peace* of an evening; a grand and consoling book—a huge panorama of life and suffering humankind which makes the present troubles easier to endure and the loneliness of death a little thing. I keep my books in a Turkish bomb-box which my servant found for me. It just holds them nicely and the transport officer will be told that it contains "messing utensils". I should be in the soup without something to read!

April 3. 9 a.m. Alone with my notebook on a thyme-scented terrace close to the camp, with the sun warming my face and large white clouds moving slowly across the blue. Bees and flies drone peacefully about the grey rocks; butterflies ramble and settle on thick white clover where a few late scarlet anemones still make a spot of colour. People tell me that the climate of Judea gets bad later on, but it is like Paradise now. A little way off an Orphean Warbler sings delightfully from a thorn bush, producing the most liquid and delicate fantasia anyone could ask for. Old vines are half hidden by the spring growth of weeds and grass. A tiny fly-catcher perches six feet away on a bush, and a red-start preens himself near by. Files of camels plod along the road far below, and limber-wheels crush the stones as they clatter along. (Eight mules to each limber.) Fig trees have a few young leaves. Clematis is over; wild roses are beginning, on big bushes. Down the hill some gunners are busy around their sixty-pounders, turning some sort of wheel with a rattling noise. I watch their tiny arms working like piston-rods. Then the unmechanical warbler begins again with a low liquid phrase, and a pair of buntings flutter on to a crab-apple tree near the ledge of rock where I'm sitting.

Then a whistle blows down by the battery; a motor bike goes along the rough road; machine-gun fire taps and echoes to crashings away among the hills—probably only practice-firing. It is a heavenly morning and a heavenly place. The war is quite subsidiary to the landscape; not a sprawling destructive monster like it is in France. Am now second-in-command of A Company. (C Company commander is back from leave.)

April 4. A hot cloudless day. Saw a lot of griffon vultures; also a flock of what the Doc. says must have been black storks, moving steadily northward—rather like aeroplanes. Wonder where they were making for.

Everyone has quite decided that we are going to France. Probably untrue.

These hills are more lovely every day with everything bursting into flower and leaf. We move down to Ludd on Sunday. I don't want to leave these hills.

Perhaps we shall return. I wonder how I should stand another dose of France. Funny to think that I *tried* to get sent there in January.

April 5. Last night after dinner (we all have it together in a big Mess Tent) there was an episode which is worth recording. The Colonel announced that he was going to have "a selling sweep on where we are going to". The procedure for a "selling sweep" was unknown to me, but there seemed to be a general notion that it was rather a dashing affair to take part in. We all sat round the table and the C.O. acted as auctioneer. First of all everyone took a ticket and then there was a "draw" and the lucky ones drew a bit of paper with a word on it. (France, Salonika, Mesopotamia, Italy, Palestine, Ireland, Submarined and Home were the words.) The whole thing put my back up properly and the C.O. looked none too pleased when I declined to take a ticket. (Now I come to think of it, it must have been the first time I've been really annoyed since I left England! The auction then started, and I must say he did it in a most lifelike manner, with appropriate witticisms delivered in flashy style. Most of the junior officers have no money except their pay, but they felt it incumbent on them to bid, either through a sycophantic desire to please, or because they dared not refuse. France fetched £15; Home £14; and Palestine £20. When he put up Submarined there was a pause, and then I bid ten pounds for it (which was my one bid during the auction). There was no advance on this and it became my exasperating property. At the end there was £94 in the pool, and France had been bought by Major Evans (Second-in-Command) who had also drawn it. (Being a thoroughly decent man he will probably pay back all the money spent by those who can't afford it.) Behind it one felt that they all dreaded going to the Western Front and would have paid anything to stay in Palestine.

It was a sort of raffish attempt to turn the whole thing into a joke and a "smart Yeomanry Regiment" gamble. Everyone knows now that we *are* going to France. All maps were handed in to-day and hot-weather kit cancelled. The M.O. evidently felt as I did, for he went quietly out before the show began.

April 7. (*Sunday.*) *6.45 a.m.* A quiet warm morning; clouds low on the hilltops and the sun shining through. Blue smoke rises from the incinerators of our camp and the one on the far side of the Nablus road. Everyone busy clearing up among the fig trees which are now misty green. To-day we begin our 45-mile march down to Ludd. It is also the first day of our journey to France, or wherever it is we are going to.

These war diaries of mine contain many a note scribbled in that hour of departure when the men are loading limbers or putting on their packs and everyone is in a fuss, except perhaps the present writer, who invariably slopes off to some secluded spot outside the camp or village. From there he hears the noise of bustling preparation—high shouts, clatter of tins, sounds of hurrying feet, "come on; fall in, headquarters"; and so on.

Birds whistle and pipe small in the still morning air, flitting among the clematis and broom, alighting on fig branches or bright green thorn bushes. The hillside feels more like a garden than ever before—an everlasting garden just outside the temporary habitations of men. In half an hour I shall be trudging along behind the column with a lot of baggage mules, trudging away from Arcadia, with not much more liberty than a mule myself.

April 7. 8 p.m. In my bivouac on a hillside near Suffa, after two days' marching. (About ten miles each day.) This morning we started from a point near Ramallah, over 3000 feet up. The early morning sky was clear; low grey banks of clouds like snow mountains above the hills toward the sea. Up at 5.15 and away by 7.40. Reached here 1.30. Passed General Allenby on the way. Hot sun and a breeze from the sea. Pink and white rock roses along the wadis. From this hill I can see a city of tiny lights below and on the opposite slope, where the rest of the Brigade are camped. Stars overhead and sound of men's voices singing and chattering: they seem contented with their lot. Away in the twilight jackals howl, and some night bird calls.

My bivouac is pitched in a tangle of large yellow daisies. (My servant is a marvel; very quiet man who never forgets anything.) A mule brays among the murmur of men's voices (probably saying what it thinks about the war). We are almost in the plains again, at the foot of the grey stony hills. Horrid smell of dead camels in places along the road this morning. Saw a Syrian Pied Woodpecker this evening. Grey with scarlet head and tail. Also a White Stork and a Hoopoe. (Doc. pointed out all three; my eyes would be useless without his help.)

Later. Reading Hardy's *Woodlanders*. Like going into a cool parlour with green reflections on wall and ceiling— after the dust and sweat of marching.

April 9. 10.45 a.m. Latron. (Exactly four weeks ago I was here on my way up.) Started 6.45 this morning. Clear dawn; its cool stillness became very hot by 8. Got here 10. Camp is on a bare sweltering slope near the dusty main road with droning lorries and files of pack animals passing. Low, rolling country, rather brown and treeless; mostly vines and corn. The sea, hazy and distant, shown by a line of sand-hills. After seeing the Company settled down I have escaped to the shadow of a thin belt of small fir trees. Tents, camps, and horse-lines only a couple of hundred yards away, but the place is cool and green, drowsy with the hum of insects and the midday chirping of a few sparrows and crested larks. Out in the vinefield, brimstone yellow with weeds, some Latronians are hoeing busily, thereby increasing my enjoyment of sitting still. Dull march to-day. Ten yards away a patriarchal person is sitting under a tree, regarding me gravely and evidently having nothing else to do. According to Old Testament topography we are now in the tribe of Dan, and I can best describe this old gent by saying that I think he looks exactly like what I think Dan ought to have looked like. After a while a welcome breeze comes from the sea, swaying the firs to an ocean murmur. Then a bird (possibly a bulbul) gives us—me and Dan— a charming flute solo. Dan dozes, and so shall I.

Evening. Out after tea, I found a charming garden beside a clear quick-flowing stream with willows and tall reeds. The garden belongs to a French monastery. Oranges, lemons, and bananas growing. Also some small apple-like fruit with large seeds in them. During a dumb-show conversation, I asked the Arab-looking gardener what these were and he said they were "askadinias" (which sounds like some sort of joke).

Came home wading through huge golden daisies among cactus-like hedges.

April 10. Up at 3.30. Started 5.30. Reached camping ground at Ludd about noon. Clear dawn with larks singing; large morning star and thin slice of moon above dim blue hills. Firefly lights of camp below.

Starting off like that in the grey-green morning is delicious. One feels so fresh, with one's long shadow swaying on, and for the first two hours the country is green and pleasant. After Ramleh (a white town with olives and fruit trees and full of British) it was very hot and the road terribly dusty. No shadow at all now and one ached all over and felt footsore—marching between cactus-hedges with motors passing all the time and clouds of dust. At lunch the C.O. told a story about some friend of his who was in charge of a camp of Turkish prisoners; they gave trouble, so he turned a machine-gun on them and killed a lot. This was received with sycophantic ha-ha's from the captains. Queer man, his lordship.

Note. Sensations of a private on the march. Left, left; left-right, left. 110 paces to the minute. Monotonous rhythm of marching beats in his brain. The column moves heavily on; dust hangs over it; dust and the glaring discomfort of the sky. Going up a hill the round steel helmets sway from side to side with the lurch of heavily-laden shoulders. Vans and lorries drone and grind and blunder along the road; cactus-hedges are caked with dust. The column passes some Turkish prisoners in dingy dark uniform and red fez, guarded by Highlanders. "Make the ——s work, Jock!" someone shouts from the ranks. . . . Through the sweat-soaked exhaustion that weighs him down, he sees and hears these things; his shoulders are a dull ache; his feet burn hot and clumsy with fatigue; his eyes are tormented by the white glare of the airless road. Men in front, men behind; no escape. "Fall out on the right of the road". . . . He collapses into a dry ditch until the whistle blows again.

Evening. April 12. Kantara. Left camp 1 p.m. yesterday with advance party. Very hot; scent of orange blossom. Train left Ludd about 5 and reached Kantara at 9 this morning. When I left here a month ago I hoped I'd seen the last of it for a long time! Felt horribly tired yesterday and wasn't much improved by sixteen hours of jolting and excruciating noise of railway truck.

Every time I woke up my face was thick with sand and grime from the engine. But it was warm, and I had my valise.

It feels positive agony to leave those Palestine hills. Here I sit, in a flapping tent close to the main road through the camp. Strong wind, and sand blowing everywhere. Nearest tree God knows where! Remainder of Battalion arrives to-morrow morning. Our party was getting tents up this morning.

After one o'clock I escaped to a lake, about a mile away in the salt marshes where nothing grows. It was quite solitary except for an aeroplane overhead and a flock of flamingoes. Kantara's tents and huts were a sand-coloured blur on the edge of the hot quivering afternoon. Blown by the wind, the water came merrily in wavelets. I had a bathe in the shallow salt water with deep mud below, and the sun and wind were quite pleasant as I ran up and down—happy, because there wasn't a soul within a mile of me, though it was a dreary sort of place when one came to think of it. Miles of flat sand; dry bushes here and there, but nothing green, and the dried mud glistening with salt. But the water was blue-green; and the flamingoes had left a few feathers on the edge of the lake before they flapped away with the light shining through their rosy wings.

April 15. 9 p.m. Another day over and wasted. Endless small tiresome details to be worried through; and at the end of the day exhaustion, exasperation, and utter inability to think clearly or collect any thoughts worth putting down.

Two men, going on leave to Cairo to-morrow, have just been into my tent for their pay; their happy excited faces the only human thing worth recording from the past 15 hours.

April 19. A week at Kantara gone by. One bad sandstorm. Company training every day 6.30-10 and in afternoon. Sand; sunlight. Haven't been half a mile from camp all the time. Last Sunday night I took a party down to get their clothes and blankets boiled. Waited 2 hours for the boilers to be disengaged, and then 100 stark naked men stood about for an hour while most of their worldly possessions were stewed.

The little Doc. goes away to-morrow to join the 10th Division who are staying in Palestine. I shall miss his bird-lore and his whimsical companionship very much.

April 23. Lying in my little bivouac (a new idea which enables me to be alone) I watch dim shapes going along the dusty white road in blue dusk and clouded moonlight. As they pass I overhear scraps of their talk. Many of them thick-voiced and full of drink. Others flit past silently. Confused shouts and laughter from the men's tents behind; from the road the sound of tramping boots. The pallor of the sand makes the sky look blue. A few stars are visible, framed in the triangle of my door, with field-glasses and haversack slung against the pole on the middle. Sometimes a horse goes by, or a rumbling lorry. So I puff my pipe and watch the world, ruminating on what exists within the narrow bivouac of my philosophy, lit by the single lantern-candle of my belief in things like *War and Peace* and *The Woodlanders*.

Since last year I seem to be getting outside of things a bit better. Recognizing the futility of war as much as ever, I dimly realize the human weakness which makes it possible. For I spend my time with people who are, most of them, too indolent-minded to think for themselves. Selfishly, I long for escape from the burden that is so much more difficult than it was two or three years ago. But the patience and simple decency which I find in the ordinary soldier, these make it possible to go on somehow. I feel sorry for them—that's what it is.

For in our Division considerably more than half the N.C.O.s and men have been on active service without leave since September 1915, when they went to Gallipoli. And now, as a nice change of air, they are being shipped back to the Western Front to help check the new German offen-

sives. Obviously they have sound reasons for feeling a bit
fed-up.

"Of course they have! That is why we are so grateful to
them and so proud of them" reply the people at home.
What *else* do they get, besides this vague gratitude? Company football matches, beer in the canteens, and one mail
in three weeks.

I felt all this very strongly a few evenings ago when a
Concert Party gave an entertainment to the troops. It
wasn't much; a canvas awning; a few footlights; two blue-
chinned actors in soft felt hats—one of them jangling rag-
time tunes on a worn-out upright; three women in short
silk skirts singing the old, old, soppy popular songs; and all
five of them doing their best with their little repertoire.

They were unconscious, it seemed to me, of the intense
impact of their audience—that dim brown moonlit mass of
men. Row beyond row, I watched those soldiers, listening
so quietly, chins propped on hands, to the songs which epitomized their "Blighty hunger", their longing for the
gaiety and sentiment of life.

In the front rows were half-lit ruddy faces and glittering
eyes; those behind sloped into dusk and indistinctness, with
here and there the glowing spark of a cigarette. And at the
back, high above the rest, a few figures were silhouetted
against the receding glimmer of the desert. And beyond
that was the starry sky. It was as though these civilians
were playing to an audience of the dead and the living—
men and ghosts who had crowded in like moths to a lamp.
One by one they had stolen back, till the crowd seemed
limitlessly extended. And there, in that half-lit oasis of
Time, they listen to "Dixieland" and "It's a long, long
trail", and "I hear you calling me". But it was the voice
of life that "joined in the chorus, boys"; and very powerful
and impressive it sounded.

*   *   *

May 1st. (*S.S. Malwa. P. & O.* 10,838 tons, after leaving
Alexandria for Marseilles. Three Battalions on board; also
Divisional General, four Brigadiers, and numerous staff-

officers. 3300 "souls" altogether not counting the boat's crew. Raft accommodation for about 1000. Six other boats in the convoy, escorted by destroyers.)

Scraps of conversation float up from the saloon below the gallery where I am sitting. "I myself believe. . . . I think, myself. . . . My own opinion is. . . ."

The speaker continues to enunciate his opinion in a rather too well-bred voice. The War—always the War— and world politics, plus a few other matters of supreme importance, are being discussed, quite informally, by a small group of staff-officers. (I know it is unreasonable, but I am prejudiced against staff-officers—they are so damned well dressed and superior!) After a while they drift away, and their superior talk is superseded by a jingle of knives, forks, and spoons; the stewards are preparing the long tables for our next meal.

S.S. Malwa (not a name that inspires confidence—I don't know why), cleaving the level water with a perturbed throbbing vibration, carries us steadily away from the un- heeding warmth and mystery of Egypt. Leaving nothing behind us, we are bound for the heavily-rumoured grim- ness of the battles in France. The troops are herded on the lower decks in stifling, dim-lit messrooms, piled and hung with litter of equipment. Unlike the Staff, they have no smart uniforms, no bottles of hair-oil, and no confidential information with which to make their chatter important and intriguing. *John Bull* and ginger beer are their chief facilities for passing the time pleasantly. They do not com- plain that the champagne on board is inferior and the food only moderate. In fact they make me feel that Dickens was right when he wrote so warm-heartedly about "the poor". They are only a part of the huge dun-coloured mass of vic- tims which passes through the shambles of war into the gloom of death where even generals "automatically revert to the rank of private". But in the patience and simplicity of their outward showing they seem like one soul. They are the tradition of human suffering and endurance, stripped of all the silly self-glorifications and embellishments by which human society seeks to justify its conventions.

May 3. I get intolerant and contemptuous about the officers on board and all that they represent. While I'm sitting in a corner reading Tolstoy (how priggish it sounds!) they come straddling in to sprawl on wicker chairs and padded seats—their faces crimson from over-drinking. Fortunately the fact that the Western Front is two thousand miles nearer Piccadilly Circus than Palestine seems to console them. But one gets an occasional glimpse of disquiet in the emergence of a haunted look or a bitter, uneasy laugh. Haunted by secret fear of what awaits them in France (plus the chance of my *Submarined* ticket winning the "selling sweep") they are to be pitied. But the pity needs to be vast, to encompass them all. No little human patronizing pity, like mine, is any use.

I too am tortured, but I begin to see that the War has re-made me and done away with a lot of my ideas that were no good. So I am really better for it, in spite of scowling bitterly at it.

Their trouble is that they can't understand why they are being made miserable by deprivation of everything in life which they want. So their suffering doesn't help them, and they hide from their despair in drinks and oblivion. And life becomes an obscene thing, as it is on this boat. Obscene terror invades the overcrowded ship when those on board awake in the morning and remember their present peril. And I wonder how many of these officers are facing the future undaunted? I mean the young ones—not the middle aged, who will be mostly safe when once ashore. I believe that there is submerged horror in their souls. They cannot think; they dare not think it out. The situation appals them. So they try to forget, and this passes for courage. Their hectic gaiety is the stuff that stimulates war-correspondents to enthusiasm.

Thus I sit and try to reason it out—evolving my notions from scraps of talk and flushed faces that are becoming gross with years of war.

Then my mental equilibrium is restored by a man I used to hunt with in Kent, who comes along and talks about the old days and what fun we used to have. But there is a look in his eyes which reminds me of something. It comes back to me quite clearly; he looked like that when he was waiting to go down to the post for his first point-to-point. And he told me afterwards that he'd been so nervous that he really didn't think he could face doing it again. And, being a shrewd sort of character, he never did.

May 4. Am still studying the psychology of the average officer on board. (Have just been wondering what Rivers would say about it.) One can only pick up surface hints and clues from talk and general behaviour, but I am inclined to suppose that they possess a protective apparatus in lazy-mindedness. "Thank goodness! Civilization again!" they murmur leaning back in a padded P. & O. chair. Cards and drinks and light fiction carry them through. Physically healthy, they know that they are "for it", and hope for a Blighty wound with a cushy job to follow. It is every man for himself. In a battle most of them would be splendid, one hopes. But army life away from the actual front is demoralizing. Remembrance of Rivers warns me against intolerance; but isn't this boat-load a sample of the human folly which can accept war as an inevitable and useful element in the routine of life? Old man Tolstoy says "the most difficult and the most meritorious thing in life is to love it in spite of all its undeserved suffering". But who cares for Tolstoy's wisdom here? Only me, apparently.

During the day I watch the men lying about on the decks in the sunlight, staring idly at the glittering glorious blue sea and the huge boats ploughing along in line—six of us, with about ten destroyers in the offing. (Coming up on deck early this morning I saw one of the destroyers firing at something, so I suppose we are being chased all the time.) Leaning against one another in indolent attitudes, the men seem much nearer the realities of life than the average officer.

I must, however, put in a word for the Divisional General, who has a very kind face and appears to be the best type of reticent regular officer. He is also reputed to be a good general. I watched him playing bridge last night in the gallery above the dining-saloon. He asked the band to

play "The Rosary" a second time. "It may be hack-
neyed," he exclaimed, "but I love it!"

May 5. In the circular gallery above the dining-saloon a
few electric lamps glow with a subdued and golden sobriety which reveals vulgar oak panelling and carved balus-
trades, bilious green curtains, and a tawdry gilt and painted
ceiling adorned with meaningless patterns. The skylight—
an atrocity in blue and green glass with the steamship
company's crest—is invisible owing to absence of light from
above, but the lunette wall spaces below are made alluring
by a pair of oleographic representations of simpering sirens
doing some dancing. Electric fans revolve and hum, hurling dim whizzing shadows on the walls like ghostly wings.
The boat throbs and quivers and creaks—straining onward
as though conscious of her own danger which keeps every
light shrouded from exterior gloom; the buzzing air is
vitiated and oppressive. The smoking-room, with its con-
vivial crowd of tipsy jabberers, is no place to write descrip-
tive prose in. Out here it is quieter. In the saloon below
some officers are playing cards; others are occupied with a
small roulette-wheel. I gaze down at their well-oiled heads,
where they bend over the green tables; I listen to the chink
of coins and the jargon of their ejaculative comments on
the game, while dusky stewards continually bring them
drinks. These are the distractions which drug their exasperation and alarm; for like the boat they are straining
forward to safety, environed by the menace of submarines.

Having watched all this for a while, I stumble from a
dim passage into blustering darkness and invigorating air.
Out there the sea is darker than the sky, but the escorting
destroyers are seen like long shadows—scarcely more than
a blur on the water, stealing forward all the time.

Gradually getting used to the gloom, I see a sentry
looming by the davits, silent above the recumbent sleepers,
while the sea races backward cavernous and chill with
spray.

All along the decks the troops are sleeping, huddled
close together under their blankets. And on their defence-
lessness a gleam of stars looks down.

Nothing is heard but the sluicing of the waves and the throb of the engines.

Within are chart-rooms and engine-rooms, and the wireless operator in his little den, and the captain in his stateroom, and all the rest of them whose dutifulness may at any moment become a futile contention with disaster. And outside, the mystery and unpitying hugeness of the sea; and the soldiers whose sleeping forms remind me of the dead.

May 7. A quiet morning with rain clouds and sunshine. We came into Marseilles harbour about 8.30 a.m. It is said that the captain of the boat celebrated our safe arrival by bursting into tears on the bridge.

May 8. Musso. (Rest camp outside Marseilles.) Yesterday afternoon we marched away from the docks at 3.15 and got here at 6.30. The troops were childishly excited by seeing a European city after being in the East so long. The bright green plane trees along the streets gave them particular pleasure. Everyone seems delighted and refreshed also by being able to read yesterday's *Daily Mail*. But it doesn't cheer me to read that "we advanced our line a little nearer Morlancourt, a position of great tactical importance". Two years ago we were living there, and it was five miles behind our Front Line.

Marseilles is a very pleasant looking place with its climbing streets and the grey hills behind. I went there this afternoon. Inspected the Zoological Gardens, as I couldn't think of anywhere else to go! Not much there, owing to the War. In one of the aviaries, among a lot of bright-plumaged little birds, there was a blackbird; looking rather the worse for wear, he sat and sang his heart out, throwing his head back and opening his yellow bill wide, quite oblivious of the others. Somehow he made me think of a prisoner of war.

May 10. (*11 p.m.*) The Battalion entrained and left Marseilles yesterday afternoon. The train has been rumbling along all day through the Rhône country, green and lovely with early summer. Now it goes on in the dark, emitting eldritch shrieks which echo along the valleys. It was a blue and white day and nightingales were singing from every bush and thicket. I hear one now, while the train has stopped, warbling in the gloom to an orchestral accompaniment of croaking frogs. Muttering voices of officers in the next compartment. In here, the other three are asleep in various ungainly attitudes. Young Howitt looks as if he were dead.

Monday, May 13. (Domvast, a village 13 k. from Abbeville.) Early yesterday morning we detrained at Noyelles, near Abbeville. On Saturday evening we were on some high ground while passing the environs of Paris. Gazing out across that city I wondered whether I shall ever go there as a civilian. It looked rather romantic and mysterious somehow, and a deep-toned bell was tolling slowly. Four hours' march from Noyelles. Got here 6.30. Into billets—farmyard smells—all just like two years ago. Weather fine, with a breeze behind us all the way. Country looking very beautiful. But May is a deceptive time of year to arrive anywhere; it creates an illusion of youth and prosperity, as though the world were trying to be friendly, and happiness somewhere ahead of one.

Domvast is a straggling village lying low among orchards with the forest of Crécy a mile away to the west. I went up there this morning in the rain. Endless avenues and vistas of green—very comforting when compared with Kantara.

I feel rather ghost-like, returning to the familiar country and happenings. Buying eggs and butter from Madame in the billets. The servants in the kitchen stammering Expeditionary Force French to the girls. The men in barns still rather pleased with their new surroundings. All the queer Arcadian business of settling down in a village still unspoilt by continuous billeting and a good 30 or 40 miles from the War.

May 14. Sitting in the Company Mess on a fine breezy afternoon copying out and assimilating a lecture on Consolidation of Captured Trenches, which I shall spout to the Company as though it came out of my head, though it is all from the recently issued *Manual for the training and employment of Platoons* which I spent yesterday evening in studying. I now feel rather "on my toes" about being in France, and am resolved to make a good job of it this time. The manual (a 32 page pamphlet) is a masterpiece of common sense, clearness, and condensation, and entirely supersedes the academic old *Infantry Training 1914* which was based on Boer War experience and caused me much mystification. Having just evolved an alliterative axiom—"clear commands create complete control"—I sit at the window watching soldiers going up and down the lane; now and then a lorry passes, or a peasant with a grey horse. On the opposite side of the road is a fine hawthorn hedge and an orchard containing two brown cows munching lush grass. A little way off, the church bell begins tolling. I tell myself that I simply must become an efficient company commander. It is the only way I can do the men any good, and they are such a decent well-behaved lot that it is a pleasure to work with them and do what one can for their comfort.

This morning we went up to the Forest and did a little training under the beech trees. "It's like being at home again, sir," one of the sergeants said to me.

It was nice to watch the groups of men under the green branches, although they were doing "gas-drill" and bayonet fighting—loathsome exercises. Nice also, to walk home a breezy mile or two with the column—the men chattering gaily and cloud shadows floating across the spacious landscape. In the hornbeam hedge on the edge of the forest a blackcap was singing, and a crow sat watching me from the young wheat.

Along that ridge, 572 years ago, the Battle of Crécy was fought!

May 15. Another golden day, fine and warm. In the afternoon we listened to the famous lecture on "The Spirit of the Bayonet". The brawny Scotchman, now a Colonel, addressed two Battalions from a farm-wagon in a bright green field. His lecture is the same as it was two years ago, but for me it fell rather flat. His bloodthirsty jokes went down well with the men, but his too-frequent references to the achievements with the bayonet of the Colonial troops were a mistake. Anyhow his preaching of the offensive spirit will have to be repeated *ad nauseam* by me in my company training perorations. Such is life!

I have just been out for a stroll in the warm dusk along twilight lanes, past farms with a few yellow-lit windows, and the glooming trees towering overhead. Nightingales were singing beautifully. Beyond the village I could see the dark masses of the copses on the hill, and the stars were showing among a few thin clouds. But the sky winked and glowed with swift flashes of the distant bombardments at Amiens and Albert, and there was a faint rumbling, low and menacing. And still the nightingales sang on. O world God made!

May 17. Took 180 men to Brigade Baths, at Nouvions. Beautiful weather, but much too far; and baths very inadequate. It was 2½ hours' march to get there, and Brigade had told us to go in full marching-order, as the Brigadier wanted the men to do plenty of route-marching. Quite a useful way of sending them to get a clean shirt! I made a row with the Adjutant and got this cancelled, which made all the difference for the troops, who quite enjoyed their outing. But their feet got soft during the journey from Egypt and the hardening process is painful!

May 18. Have just been down the lane to see the Company Sergeant-Major about the armourer inspecting rifles. I feel very paternal when I watch the men sitting about outside their barn—gobbling stew out of canteen-lids, scribbling letters, chattering and smoking or lying asleep in the long grass under the apple-trees, while blankets are spread out everywhere to dry and old shirts and socks hung on currant bushes after being washed. The two company cooks, begrimed and busy with the "cooker", and the orderly sergeant making a list of something on a packing-case. (The Quartermaster's stores are in our yard.)

Some of them look up as I pick my way among them. I think they begin to realize that I am doing my best for them.

I am now "censoring" some of their letters, so I will transcribe a few typical extracts.

1. "Well, lad, this is a top-hole country, some difference to Palestine. It gives a chap a new inside to see some fields and hedges again. Just like old Blighty! . . . There is great talk of leave just now. In fact a party goes to-morrow.

Time-expired men first. I'm a *duration* man. What hopes! Never mind, Cheer-oh!"

2. "Well dear I dont sea any sighn of my leave but if we dont get it soon it will be a grate disapointment to us all for we all expected to get one when we came to England."

3. "The weather has been lovely since I came here: we are nowhere near the line yet. I've been going to the doctor these last few days, *sore feet*, so all I do now is going round these farms buying eggs for myself, so you see I'm not doing so bad."

Sunday. May 19. People send me the weekly reviews from England, but reading political journalism doesn't make much impression on my mind. Life is conditioned by the effort of campaigning, and I can see no further than the moment when I have got this Company back from its first "show" on the Western Front. All my efforts are centred on that, and I have, for the time being, escaped from my own individuality (except when I am writing my diary!) This is not a bad state to arrive at. War has its compensa- tions—for the conscientious officer! . . .

Written as I lie on my bed after lunch. Mice trickling about among the kit strewn on the dusty floor of this ram- shackle room with its musty old cupboards, in which the mice live among old black dresses and other rubbish. Handsome Howitt asleep on the floor, with his moody sensual face and large limbs. (As usual he looks as if he were dead.) He is a shy, simple, rather uncouth boy— brave and reliable, I foresee.

"Stiffy" Roberts, the other 19-year-old officer, is stocky and self-possessed and full of fun. Both are inclined to indo- lence, but very good lads. The other platoon commander is Harry Jones; nearly 40, clean-shaven and saturnine and fluent with jokes and stories. Has knocked about the world, in East Africa and Cardiff. Result—a ruined digestion and a lot of good sense. A knowing old bird. Am not sure how much he can be trusted. Our fourth officer is on leave. (Promoted from the ranks and not very promising.)

Later. It is now 5.30 and I have left them all scribbling down the notes on training which I've given them. The sun blazes from a clear sky; in the orchard where I am sitting the trees begin to lengthen their shadows on the green and gold and white floor of grass, buttercups, and daisies. Aeroplanes drone overhead; but the late afternoon is full of tranquillity and beauty. No one can take this loveliness from my heart.

May 20. This afternoon we marched over to Cauchy, a couple of miles away; hot sun; green wheat, and barley and clover; occasional whiffs of hawthorn smell along the narrow lanes; two red may trees over a wall, and the hawthorn whitening the landscape everywhere.

Our Brigade formed a hollow square on the green hillside above the red-roofed village snug among its trees. The Brigadier stalked on to the scene, followed by the modest Major-General who received the salute of a small forest of flashing bayonets. The General, speaking loud and distinct but rather fast, told us that he'd never been more honoured, proud, and pleased than to-day when he had come to do honour to one of the most gallant men he'd ever known. He felt sure we were all equally proud and honoured. (The men had come along using awful language owing to their having been turned out for this show before they'd finished their midday meal.) He then read out the exploits which had won Corporal Whiteway the V.C. Nothing was finer in the whole history of the British Army. The Corporal had captured a machine-gun post single-handed, shot and bayonetted the whole team (who were Turks) and redeemed the situation on his Battalion front. The General then called for Corporal Whiteway (of the Shropshire Light Infantry) and a clumsily-built squat figure in a round steel helmet doubled out of the front rank of his Company, halted, and saluted. The General then pinned something on his breast (after dropping the pin, which the Brigade-Major adroitly recovered from the long grass). He then, in a loud voice, wished Whiteway a long and happy life in which to wear his decoration, and wrung him by the hand. The little Corporal turned about and was hurriedly escaping to the shelter of the bayonet-forest, but was called back to stand beside the General who called for the General

Salute—"to do honour to Whiteway" Three cheers were
then given, and that was, officially, the end of the Turkish
machine-gun team till the Day of Judgment.

No doubt the deed was magnificent, but the spectacle
wasn't impressive.

One felt it was all done to raise the morale of the troops.
The Army is kept together by such stunts. . . . There is a
"General Routine Order" which reads as follows: "It has
been ruled by the Army Council that the act of voluntarily
supplying blood for transfusion to a comrade, although ex-
emplifying self-sacrifice and devotion, does not fall within
the qualification 'Acts of gallantry or distinguished con-
duct'." In other words, blood must be spilt, not transfused.
But I am bound to admit that the bayonet fighting lecture
and this V.C. parade have had a stimulating effect on the
troops. Good weather, rations, and billets have been even
better aids to morale, however!

I sometimes wonder whether this diary is worth writing.
But there can't be any harm in the truth, can there? And
my diary is the only person I can talk to quite openly.

May 21. Another cloudless day. In the morning I lec-
tured the Company for fifteen minutes on "Morale and
Offensive Spirit". Couldn't help thinking how amused
Rivers would have been if he'd been there. What wouldn't
I give for an hour with him now! (But the test is that I've
got to get through it all without him.) After tea I gave the
senior N.C.O.s a forty-minute talk under the apple-trees,
and really felt as if I were quite a good instructor. The feeling that they like and trust me "gives me a new inside".
And I have this advantage, that my predecessor was dead-
stale and not at all active-minded. So these splendid
N.C.O.s respond to what I try to tell them and are really
keen. After lunch we did two hours (full marching order)
in the forest. Very pleasant in there among the green glory
of the beeches with sunshine filtering through. Prolonged
wearing of gas-masks in company training rather trying.
It is now 10.30 on a moonlight night with hawthorn scents
and glimmerings and nightingale songs. The Boches are
overhead, dropping bombs on neighbouring villages. Shat-

tering din and organ-drone of planes going on now. They
have been hammering Abbeville heavily lately. Sleeping
badly lately, but nothing matters except the Company.

May 22. Cloudless weather again. Quiet day's training.
Yesterday I began to read Duhamel's *Vie des Martyres* (a
grand book well translated). I expect *he* felt he was in a
groove while he wrote it—patiently studying the little
world of his hospital with such immense compassion. While
reading I suddenly realized the narrowness of the life a soldier leads on active service.

The better the soldier, the more limited is his outlook.

I am learning to understand soldiers and their ideas; intelligent instruction of them teaches me a lot. But I find
them very difficult to put on paper. And in these days of
hawthorn blossom and young leaves they seem like a part
of the passing of the year. Autumn will bring many of them
to oblivion. "It is written that you should suffer without
purpose and without hope. But I will not let all your sufferings be lost in the abyss," wrote Duhamel. That is how I
feel too; but all I can do for them is to try and obtain them
fresh vegetables with my own money, and teach them how
to consolidate shell-holes, and tell them that "the soul of
defence lies in offence"!

To-morrow morning we leave Domvast. Somewhere between Arras and St. Pol will be our area for "intensive
training".

Magnicourt. May 24. "Yesterday" began at 2.30 a.m.
and ended at 11 p.m. when the Company were safely
settled down in billets after 20 miles' marching and 5 hours
in the train. (Covered trucks.) We marched away from
Domvast at 5 a.m. A warm, still morning with a quiet sunrise glinting behind us beyond the trees and the village.
Crossing the Abbeville-St. Omer road, we went through
Crécy Forest for about 8 miles. There had been some rain
in the night and the air smelt of damp leaves and dust.

Entrained at Rue, one o'clock, and reached St. Pol
about 6.30. Marched 5 miles to billets. Strong breeze;
much colder. It has rained all to-day and the men have
been resting (the whole Company in one huge lofty barn,

with nice clean straw). I have got a room up a lane, with churchyard view (!) and a clock ticking peacefully on a shelf. Have just received orders to move again to-morrow.

Sitting here I glance over my right shoulder at the little row of books, red and green and blue, which stand waiting for my hand, offering their accumulated riches. I think of the years that *may* be in store for me, and of all the pages I *may* turn. Then I look out at the falling rain and the grey evening beyond the churchyard wall and wonder if anything awaits me that will be more truly human than my sense of satisfaction yesterday at Rue railway station. What did I do to gain that feeling? . . . There were five of my men who had come too late to get any tea. Disconsolately they stood at the empty dixy—tired out by the long march and herded into a dirty van to be carried a bit nearer to hell. But I managed to get some hot tea for them. Alone I did it. Without me they would have got none. And for the moment the War seemed worth while! . . . That sort of thing reminds me of my servant and the numberless small worries and exasperations which he has saved me from in the past ten weeks. Nothing could be better than the way he does things, quiet and untiring. He is simple, humble, patient, and brave. He is reticent yet humorous. How many of us can claim to possess these qualities and ask no reward but a smile? It might have been of him that Duhamel wrote—"he waged his own war with the divine patience of a man who had waged the great world-war, and who knows that victory will not come right away." His name is 355642 Pte. John Bond. I write it here in case I am killed.

Little ginger-haired Clements, our shy Company clerk, who works so hard, goes home for a month's leave to-morrow. Funny to think that some of us may be dead when he comes back to his documents and "returns". About 150 strong and healthy men, all wondering how soon they'll get killed and hoping it will be someone else. Obvious, I suppose, but a peculiar notion to have in one's head!

May 25. Habarcq. (12 k. from Arras.) We left Magnicourt at 9 a.m. Warm day. Beastly march of ten miles;

very slow, owing to congestion of troops. This is a large village but very much overcrowded with troops.

A girl watching us pass through a village to-day cried out in astonishment—"*Ne pas des anciens!*" We certainly are a fine body of men.

One of our platoons is billeted close to a burial ground, which they refer to as "the rest camp". "No reveilles and route-marches there!" remarked a tall, tired-looking man with a walrus moustache. Getting near the line is working me up into the same old feeling of confidence and freedom from looking far ahead. Is it self-defensive, or what?

Sunday, May 26. Very tired to-night. Guns making a noise eight miles away. I am alone in a large room in the Château—a barrack of a place. Small things have conspired to exasperate me to-day. But I will read *Lamb's Letters* and then go to sleep. My window looks out on tree-tops and a large cedar. (I am on the third storey.)

May 28. Too tired to read or think after two days' hard work with the Company. Devilish noise last night when the next village was being bombed and anti-aircraft guns firing. They are over again to-night.

May 29. Inspection by Divisional General. He made a very pleasant impression, and talked very nicely to the men. No complaints about my Company, anyhow! . . . Letters from England seem to come from another world. Aunt Evelyn wants to know when I shall be coming home on leave. Damn leave; I don't want it. And I don't want to be wounded and wangle a job at home. I want the next six weeks, and success. Do I want death? I don't know yet. Anyhow the War is outside of life, and I'm in the War. "Those we loved were merely happy shadows." (Duhamel again.)

Sunday, June 2. Cloudless weather continues. On Friday I took the Company to fire on the range; eight miles each way; out 7.30 to 6. Fired five rounds myself; a bull's-eye, two inners, and a magpie were duly signalled. My private opinion is that I never hit the target at all, and I rather think the Sergeant-Major winked at me when handing me the rifle!

Yesterday we paraded at 6 a.m. and went seven miles to take part in a Brigade Field Day. Back at 4.30. The men's feet are very much knocked about and boots getting bad. I keep on worrying the Quartermaster about it, but he can do nothing except "indent" for boots which never arrive. Morale of Company very good, in spite of being put through it so intensively. Only three have gone on leave since we got to France. One goes next week; and the rest are *hoping*.

This morning at 8.30 I was shaving (up before 5 the last two days). Below my window a voluntary service was in progress, and about 20 voices struck up dolefully with "How sweet the name of Jesus sounds". It seemed funny, somehow—Jesus being a name which crops up fairly often on Brigade Field Days and elsewhere! Later on the Padre was preaching about the "spiritual experiences of the righteous".

After breakfast I sat under the apple-blossom behind our Mess and read a Homeric Ode to Hermes (not in Greek). It felt a great relief after a week of incessant toil over small details. But it was only a half-hour's respite from being worried by the Orderly Room. Anyhow I feel strong and confident in the security of a sort of St. Martin's Summer of Happy-Warriorism. We are now on G.H.Q. Reserve and liable to move at 24-hours' notice.

After a hasty lunch I spent $1\frac{1}{2}$ hours at a "Company Officers' Conference" and listened to a lecture on Trench Warfare and a discussion of yesterday's Field Day. The Brigadier has warned us to expect "the fall of Paris". (The Germans are on the Marne and claim 45,000 more prisoners.)

But I have my large airy upper-chamber in the Château where I can be alone sometimes. From the window one sees the tops of big trees; a huge cedar, two fine ashes, a walnut, and some chestnuts. All towering up very magnificently. Birds chirp; the guns rumble miles away; and my servant has picked some syringa and wild roses, which are in a bowl by my bed. A jolly young lance-corporal (headquarters signaller) came in to cut my hair this morning; he chattered away about the Germans and so on. Likes

France, but thinks the War can't be ended by fighting. Very sensible. Then he clattered down the stairs (echoing boards) whistling "Dixieland".

After tea the mail came in; a good one for me as it contained de la Mare's new book of poems. I went out and read some of them under a thorn hedge, sitting in the long grass with a charming glimpse of the backs of barns and men sitting in the sun, and the graveyard. All the graves are of men killed in the war—mostly French. But there are flowers—white pinks and pansies.

Then I watched the Company playing football, and getting beaten. And now I must do the accounts of our Company mess.

June 4. Out 7.15 till 4.15. Did a Battalion attack. After lunch a gas lecture, and then we were bombarded with smoke and gas. I was feeling jumpy and nerve-ridden all day. It would be a relief to shed tears now. But I smoke on my bed, and the Divisional brass band is tootling on the grass outside the Château.

I will read de la Mare and try to escape from feeling that after all I am nothing but what the Brigadier calls "a potential killer of Huns". . . .

> *Beyond the rumour even of Paradise come,*
> *There, out of all remembrance, make our home.*

*   *   *

June 5. (*9.30 p.m.*) Yesterday was the first bad day I've had for several weeks and I finished up feeling terribly nervy. This morning I got up, with great difficulty, at 6.30, and at 7.45 we started out for a Brigade Field Day. Did an attack from 10.30 to 2.30, but it wasn't a strenuous one for me as I was told to "become a casualty" soon after the 3000-yard assault began, and I managed to make my way unobtrusively to an old windmill on a ridge near by. There I lay low as long as I dared, and thoroughly enjoyed myself. Below the hill I could see the troops advancing by rushes over the rye-grass of some luckless farmer. Larks were singing overhead and the sunlit countryside was swept by the coursing shadows of great white clouds. I'd escaped

from soldiering for an hour, and was utterly content to sit
up there among the rafters, watching the beams that filtered through chinks and listening to the creaking silence
—alone in that place which smelt of old harvests, and where
the rumour of war was a low rumble of guns, very far
away. So I am in good spirits again this evening, and my
nerve-furies have sailed away into the blue air.

When I rode into the transport-lines this afternoon I saw
young Stonethwaite drudging at cleaning a limber, super-
vised by a military policeman.

He has still got ten days to do, of his 28 days "Field
Punishment No. 2" for coming on parade drunk at Marseilles. I gave him a cheery nod and a grin, and he smiled
back at me as he stood there in his grimy slacks and blue
jersey. I hadn't spoken to him since I "talked to him like a
father" when he was awaiting his court martial. He was in
the other Company I was with for a time in Palestine, and
I took an interest in him, partly because he'd served with
our First Battalion in France, and partly because of the
noticeably nice look in his face. (He was the sort of chap
that no one could help liking.) There was something purposeful and promising about him, even when he was only
sitting on a rock in Judea trying to mend one of his rotten
boots. I remember watching him playing football at Kantara, and he seemed the embodiment of youthful enter-
prise. But some of the old toughs got him blind to the world
at Marseilles, and when I heard about it I felt quite miserable. So I went into the shed at Domvast where he was shut
up and talked to him about making a fresh start and so on.
And I suppose he felt grateful to me, standing there with
his white face and his eyes full of tears. Seeing him there
this afternoon I felt very glad I'd been kind to him. And he
is being transferred to the Machine-Gun Corps, where he
can begin all over again and be as popular as ever. I mention this little story because it has struck me as such a contrast to that V.C. investment parade.

June 6. (*10.30 p.m.*) Was summoned this evening to an
emergency meeting of Company officers in the Colonel's
room downstairs.

Large gloomy room, not much lit by a few candles.

C.O., sitting at the end of a long table, looking solemn and portentous, broke the news to us that we are shortly to take over the Neuville-Vitasse sector from the Second Canadian Division. He spoke in hushed tones (as though the Germans might overhear him). As I sat there I thought of the "selling sweep", to which this seemed a natural sequel! Anyhow I am going up to the line for three days tomorrow, with the C.O. and one of the other Company Commanders, to obtain a little experience of the sector we shall take over, and ought to be able to find out quite a lot.

June 8. (In the Front Line, near Mercatel.) Yesterday morning, in fine weather, we rode to Avesnes, and were conveyed thence in a lorry to Basseux (which was the last billet I was in with the Second Battalion). Then on to Agny and lunched at Brigade H.Q. Two mile walk from there up to Battalion H.Q. The devastated area looking dried-up and as devastated as ever. Canadian Colonel with a V.C.— evidently a terrific fire-eater but very pleasant. A guide brought me up to B Company H.Q. in the Front Line, which I reached about 7.30. The Company Commander, Captain Duclos, has been wounded twice and in France 21 months. If he gets one more "Blighty" he'll stay there, he says. In spite of his name he speaks no French but many of his company are from Quebec and speak very little English.

There was a fair amount of shelling last evening; considerable patrolling activity on our side, and much sending up of flares by the Boche. In fact things are much the same as they used to be, except that we didn't sniff for mustard-gas then, and didn't walk about with "box-respirators in the alert position". I don't think I'm any worse than I was at Fricourt and Mametz. I would have enjoyed doing a patrol last night. But I feel a bit of a fool being up here with no responsibility for anything that happens, so it is rather a good test of one's nerves.

These trenches are narrow and not sandbagged. They will be very wet when it rains. At present they are as dry as dust. Very few rats. Company H.Q. is in a steel hut which would just stop a whizz-bang.

Duclos seems a fine chap. He was very friendly last night, and we sat and jawed about old battles and cursed the politicians and the people with cushy jobs—all the usual dug-out talk. And I went to sleep at stand-to (2.30) and woke with the usual trench mouth.

Odd that I should find myself back here, only a mile or two away from where I was wounded (and the Front Line a mile or two farther back after 14 months' fighting!).

I have returned into the past, but none of my old friends are here. I am looking across to the ridge where Ormand and Dunning and all those others were killed. Nothing can bring them back; and I come blundering into it all again to guffaw with a Canadian captain. The old crowd are gone; but young "Stiffy" and Howitt are just as good.

Expect I'll see more than enough of this sector, so I won't describe it in detail. The landscape is the deadly conventional Armageddon type. Low green-grey ridges fringed with a few isolated trees, half smashed; a broken wall here and there—straggling dull-grey silhouettes which were once French villages. Then there are open spaces broken only by ruined wire-tangles, old trenches, and the dismal remains of an occasional rest camp of huts. The June grass waves, poppies flame, shrapnel bursts in black puffs, an aeroplane drones, larks sing, and someone comes along the trench clinking a petrol tin (now used for water). And this is about all one sees as one stumps along the communication-trenches, dry and crumbling and chalky, with a dead mole lying about here and there.

*   *   *

Inside Company H.Q. I watch another conventional trench-warfare scene. Duclos snores on his wire-netting berth, while I sit at a table with one large yellow candle burning. On the table is a grease-spotted sheet of *The Sussex Express*. Heaven knows why it got here, but it enables me to read "Whist Drive at Heathfield" and "Weak Milk at Hellingly", and indulge in a few "free associations" about Sussex. At the other end of the tubular steel Nissen hut, daylight comes unnaturally through the door;

evening sunshine. The H.Q. runner, a boy of 19, leans
against the door-post, steel hat tilted over his eyes and long
eyelashes showing against the light. The signaller sits at a
table with his back to me, making a gnat-like noise on his
instrument. The servants are cooking, with sandbags
soaked in candle-grease, and this typical smell completes
the picture! From outside one hears dull bumpings of artillery and the leisurely trickle of shells passing overhead.
Now and then the tap-tap of machine-gun fire. . . .

(*After midnight.*) Went out about 10 and dropped in for
an unpleasant half-hour. The Germans put over a "box-
barrage" including a lot of aerial torpedoes. No gas, however. The Battalion on our left were raided, and the uproar
was hideous. When it was all over I came back here and
read *Lamb's Letters*, which I'd brought with me as an antidote to such performances. I was much impressed by
Duclos during the "strafe". He knows just how to walk
along a trench when everything feels topsy-turvy and the
semi-darkness is full of booms and flashes. He never hur-
ries; quietly, with (one imagines) a wise, half-humorous
look masking solid determination and mastery of the situation, he moves from sentry to sentry; now getting up on the
fire-step to lean over beside some scared youngster who
peers irresolutely into the drifting smoke which hides the
wire where the Germans may be lying, ready to rush forward; now cracking a joke with some grim old soldier.
"Everything Jake here?" he asks, going from post to post,
always making for the place where the din seems loudest,
and always leaving a sense of security in his wake. Men
finger their bayonets and pull themselves together when
his cigarette-end glows in the dusk, a little planet of un-
quenchable devotion to duty.

Sunday, June 9. I left the Front Line at 3 o'clock this afternoon. Two killed and eight wounded last night. Coming
down the communication-trench I passed two men carrying a dead body slung on a pole. "What's the weight of
your pig?" asked a man who met them, squeezing himself
against the side of the trench to let them pass. Colonial
realism!

After various delays I got back to Habarcq at 11 p.m. and here I am in my quiet room again, with the trees rustling outside and a very distinct series of War pictures in my head. The businesslike futility of it is amazing. But those Canadians were holding their sector magnificently, and gave me a fine object-lesson in trench-organization.

June 13. Too busy to write anything lately. I seem to be on my legs all the time. On Tuesday we did an attack with Tanks, Sitting on the back of a Tank, joy-riding across the wheat in afternoon sunshine, I felt as if it were all rather fun—like the chorus of haymakers in the opening scene of a melodrama! But when I see my 150 men on parade, with their brown healthy faces, and when I watch them doing their training exercises or marching sturdily along the roads, I sometimes think of what may be awaiting them. (Only a couple of weeks ago one of our best Service Battalions was practically wiped out in the fighting on the Aisne.) And so (to quote Duhamel again) I "realize the misery of the times and the magnitude of their sacrifice."

I have never seen such a well-behaved company. But when their day's work is over they have about four hours left, with nothing to do and nowhere to go except the estaminets. I calculate that about £500 a week is spent, by our Battalion alone, in the estaminets of this village, and every man goes to bed in varying degrees of intoxication! What else can they do, when there isn't so much as a Y.M.C.A. hut in the place? They aren't fond of reading, as I am!

Every night I come back to my big empty room, where the noise of bombardments miles away is like furniture being moved about overhead. And from 8.30 to 10.30 I read and do my day's thinking. Often I am too tired to think at all, and am pursued by worries about Lewis guns and small company details. And while I'm reading some-one probably drops in for a talk and I must put down *Motley and Other Poems* and listen to somebody else's grumbles about the War (and Battalion arrangements).

Outside, the wind hushes the huge leafy trees; and I wake early and hear the chorus of birds through half-dissolved veils of sleep. But they only mean another day of harsh realities which wear me down.

It isn't easy to be a company commander with a suppressed "anti-war complex"! When I was out here as a platoon commander I was able to indulge in a fair amount of day-dreaming. But since I've been with this Battalion responsibility has been pushed on to me, and since we've been in France I haven't often allowed myself to relax my efforts to be efficient. Now that our intensive training is nearly finished I am easing off a bit and allowing myself to enjoy books. The result is that I immediately lose my grip on soldiering and begin to find everything intolerable except my interest in the welfare of the men. One cannot be a useful officer and a reader of imaginative literature at the same time. Efficiency depends on attention to a multitude of minor details. I shall find it easier when we get to the Line, where one alternates between intense concentration on real warfare and excusable recuperation afterwards. Here one is incessantly sniped at by the Orderly Room and everyone is being chivvied by the person above him. I have never been healthier in body than I am now. But under that mask of physical fitness the mind struggles and rebels against being denied its rights. The mechanical stupidity of infantry soldiering is the antithesis of intelligent thinking.

Sensitive and gifted people of all nations are enduring some such mental starvation in order to safeguard—whatever it is they are told that they are safeguarding. . . . And O, how I long for a good Symphony Concert! The mere thought of it is to get a glimpse of heaven.

June 14. At dinner this evening I was arguing with young "Stiffy", who has strong convictions of his own infallibility. But it was only about some detail of Lewis-gun training! Also he asserted that I'd got "a downer" on some N.C.O., which I stoutly denied. We got quite hot over it. Then the argument dissolved into jollity and fled from our minds for ever. After all, we'd had a good feed, and some red wine; to-morrow will be Saturday, an easy day's work; and the others had come in to the meal flushed and happy after a platoon football match. "Damn it, I'm fed up with all this training!" I exclaimed in a loud voice, scrooping back my chair on the brick floor and standing up. "I want to go up to the Line and really do something," added I—quite the dare-devil.

"Same here", agreed handsome boy Howitt in his soft voice. Howitt always agrees with me. He is gentle and un-assuming and not easily roused, but he gets things done. "Stiffy" is thick-set and over-confident and inclined to contradict his elders, but good-natured.

I went out into the cool, grey, breezy evening. Miles away the guns muttered and rumbled as usual. "Come on, then; come on, you poor fool!" they seemed to be saying. I shivered, and came quickly up to the Château—to this quiet room where I spend my evenings ruminating and trying to tell myself the truth—this room where I become my real self, and feel omnipotent while reading Tolstoy and Walt Whitman (who had very little in common, I sup-pose, except their patriarchal beards). "I want to go up to the Line and really do something!" I had boasted thus in a moment of vin rouge elation, catching my mood from those lads who look to me as their leader. How should they know the shallowness of my words? They see me in the daylight of my activities, when I must acquiesce in the evil that is war. But in the darkness where I am alone my soul rebels against what we are doing. "Stiffy", grey-eyed and sen-sible and shrewd; Howitt, dark-eyed and loverlike and thoughtful; how long have you to live—you in the plenitude of youth, in your pride of being alive, your ignorance of life's narrowing and disillusioning road? It may be that I shall live to remember you as I remember all those others who were my companions for a while and whose names are no longer printed in the Army List. What can I do to defeat the injustice which claims you, perhaps, as victims, as it claimed those ghostly others? Sitting here with my one candle I know that I can do nothing. "Save his own soul he has no star."

PART FOUR: FINAL EXPERIENCES

I

I never went back to those trenches in front of Neuville-Vitasse.

The influenza epidemic defied all operation orders of the Divisional staff, and during the latter part of June more than half the men in our brigade were too ill to leave their billets. Owing to the fact that I began a new notebook after June 14th, and subsequently lost it, no contemporary record of my sensations and ideas is available; so I must now write the remainder of this story out of my head.

The first episode which memory recovers from this un-diaried period is a pleasant one. I acquired a second-in-command for my company.

Hitherto no such person had existed, and I was beginning to feel the strain. In that private life of mine which more or less emerges from my diary, solemn introspection was getting the better of my sense of humour.

But now a beneficent presence arrived in the shape of Velmore, and I very soon began to say to myself that I really didn't know what I'd have done without him. It was like having an extra head and a duplicate pair of eyes. Velmore was a tall, dark, young man who had been up at Oxford for an academic year when the outbreak of war interrupted his studies. More scholastic than soldier-like in appearance (mainly because he wore spectacles) he had the look of one who might some day occupy a professorial chair. His previous experience at the front gave him a solid basis of usefulness, and to this was added a temperament in which kindliness, humour, and intelligence divided the honours equally, with gentleness and modesty in readiness to assert themselves by the power of non-assertion.

With these valuable qualities he combined—to my

astonishment and delight—what in conventional military
circles might have been described as "an almost rabid love
of literature". To hear poetry talked about in our company
mess was indeed a new experience for me. But Velmore, on
his very first evening, calmly produced Flecker's poems
from his pocket and asked young "Stiffy" if he had ever
read *The Golden Journey to Samarkand*. When he volunteered
to read some of it aloud the junior officers exchanged em-
barrassed glances and took an early opportunity to leave
me alone with my second-in-command, who was soon
enunciating, with ingratiating gusto:

> *Across the vast blue shadow-sweeping plain*
> *The gathered armies darken through the grain*
> *Swinging curved swords and dragon-sculptured spears,*
> *Footmen, and tiger-hearted cavaliers.*

A paraphrase of the last two lines became Velmore's
stock joke when reporting that the company was on parade
and it was a great consolation to me to hear that fine body
of men described as "the footmen with their dragon-sculp-
tured spears". But Velmore was never anything else but a
consolation to me.

With an all-pervading sense of relief I used to smoke my
pipe and watch him doing the office-work for me. Whenever an automatic annoyance arrived from Orderly Room
I merely passed it on and he squared it up with facetious
efficiency.

In the fourth year of the war the amount of general information which descended on us from higher quarters had
become prodigious. But I no longer received it seriously
now. Corps H.Q. could send along anything it chose and
Orderly Room forward it on for my "necessary attention"
but until Velmore decided that it was worth looking at, I
allowed it to be superseded by the next consignment of
"hot air" from those who were such experts at putting
things on paper.

Toward the end of June we moved north. I can remember that Velmore, on a fat cob, ambled away in advance of
us to act as brigade billeting officer. Our destination was

St. Hilaire, a village near Lillers, and I know that we were there on July 1st. This information is obtained from an army notebook which has accidentally survived destruction. My final entry in the company messing accounts reads as follows: "*St. Hilaire, July 1st. Rent of Mess. 24 francs. Sardines, etc. 41 francs.*" Not much to go on, is it? . . . Sardines, etc. . . . Those sardines never suspected that they would one day appear in print.

The influenza epidemic having blown over, we were now feeling fairly well tuned up for our first tour of trenches in France. As far as my own career was concerned it certainly seemed to be about time to be up and doing, for it was now fully seven months since my dim and distant medical board, and my offensiveness toward the enemy had so far been restricted to telling other people how to behave offensively when a future effort was required of them. On July 7th we were still awaiting the order to move up to the Line. It was a Sunday, and there was a church parade for the whole battalion. This was a special occasion, for we were addressed by a bishop in uniform, a fact which speaks for itself.

In a spare notebook I wrote down the main points of his sermon, so I am able to transcribe what might otherwise appear to be inaccurately remembered.

"The bishop began by saying how very proud and very pleased he was to have the privilege of welcoming us to the Western Front on behalf of his branch of the service. Every heart, he said, had thrilled with pride when the news came that our Division had captured Jerusalem. The armies in France had been enthusiastic about it. He then gave us the following information, speaking with stimulating heartiness, as one having authority from a Higher Quarter.

"(1) Owing to the Russian Revolution the Germans have got the initiative and are hammering us hard.

"(2) The troops are more enthusiastic about winning the War than they were last year. Our lads feel that they'd rather die than see their own land treated like Belgium.

"(3) It is religion which keeps the morale of the British Army so high.

"(4) (With extreme unction.) Thank God we hold the seas!

"(5) The Americans are coming across in large numbers.

"(6) A distinguished general told me last week that the Huns are getting weaker every week. Time is on our side!

"He then preached a bit about the spiritual aspects and implications of the labours, dangers, and sufferings of which we were about to partake.

"Great was the sacrifice, but it was supremely glorious. He compared us to the early Christians who were burnt alive and thrown to the lions. 'You must not forget' he added, 'that Christ is not the effete figure in stained-glass windows but the Warrior Son of God who moves among the troops and urges them to yet further efforts of sacrifice.'

"He concluded impressively by reciting, with lifted hand, two verses from the American hymn *God goes marching on*. Except, perhaps, for the early Christian comparison, the troops rather liked it."

Talking to Velmore (whose eye I had resolutely avoided during the oration) I remarked that it was the spiritual equivalent of Campbell's bayonet fighting lecture, and I still think that I was somewhere near the truth. It was the bishop's business to say that sort of thing to the troops, and no one was any the worse for it—least of all himself, for I never saw a man who looked more pink and well-nourished. Would he talk like that again, I wonder, if he got another chance?

Anyhow his optimism was confined to the immediate present and did not include the pluperfect future. What he should have said was, "We are going on with this War because we ruddy well don't intend to be beaten by the Germans. And I am here because I believe in keeping religion in touch with the iniquitous methods by which nations settle their disputes. And you are here to try and prevent it happening again." But when he told us that the Huns were getting weaker every week, not a man in the battalion believed him. They had heard that sort of thing too often before.

If he had told us that the War would end in four months' time we should have charitably assumed that he was suffering from martial religious mania. In July 1918 everyone took it for granted that we should hold on till the winter and then wait for the "1919 offensive" which staff-officers on the boat from Alexandria had discussed with such professional earnestness. It is worth remembering that the German collapse in the autumn came as a complete surprise to the armies in France. They knew nothing and had become extremely sceptical about everything they were told.

On that fine summer morning the bishop, like a one-armed sign-post pointing westward, directed us on the road to victory. But he did it without knowing that his optimism was to be justified by future events.

II

The village of St. Hilaire was at that time about nine miles from the line to which the British army had retreated during the German offensive in April. In the late afternoon of the following day I found myself riding up there on the company charger, a quadruped who has left me no describable memory, except that he suffered from string-halt and his hind-leg action was the only lively thing about him. Well primed with map-references and urgent instructions from Orderly Room, I was going up to obtain all possible information from the battalion we were to relieve next day. Jogging along the pavé road from Lillers to St. Venant I felt agreeably excited, though anxious lest I might fail to grasp (and jot down) the entire situation when I arrived there. As was usual in such emergencies, I assumed that everything would go wrong with the "relief" if I made the slightest mistake, and I felt no certainty that I could achieve what I had been told to do. It did not occur to my simple mind that by to-morrow afternoon our quartermaster would probably know quite as much about the essential facts as I should. Details of organization in the army always scared and over-impressed me. Such things seemed so much easier when one was actually doing them than when they were being conferred about and put on paper in the mysterious language of the military profession.

This anxious devotion to duty probably prevented me from acquiring a permanent mental picture of my surroundings while I was nearing the end of my ride. The fact remains that I can now only see myself as "a solitary horseman" crossing the La Bassée Canal in the dusk and then going on another two miles to battalion headquarters, which were in what appeared to be a fairly well-preserved farmhouse. There I was given food, drink, and technical enlightenment, and sent on to the Front Line.

Communication-trenches were non-existent. My guide led me along a footpath among damaged crops and looming willows, past the dug-outs of the support-company, until we arrived at an enormous shell-hole which contained a company headquarters. In a sort of rabbit-hole, with just enough room for three people in it, I was welcomed by two East Lancashire officers, and forthwith I scribbled five pages of rough notes in my Field Message Book. I could reproduce these notes in full, for the book is on my table now; but I will restrict myself to a single entry.

"Battalion code-word. ELU. No messages by buzzer except through an officer. Relief word. JAMA. (To be confirmed by runner.)" "To be confirmed by rumour" was what I actually thought as I wrote it down, but I kept the witticism to myself as the captain didn't look likely to be amused by it. He seemed a bit fussed, which caused me to feel rather confident and efficient in an unobtrusive way.

He was a decent little chap, and I got a laugh out of him by telling him that a bishop had told our battalion, only yesterday, that the Huns were getting weaker every week. Over a mug of tea he confided in me that his company would be doing a small raid, in about half an hour, and he was evidently worrying about it, though he didn't say so.

This, however, was more in my line than scribbling down what time water cart would be sent up to ration dump and how many food-containers and water tins would be taken over from out-going battalion, and it seemed much more to the point when I followed him up to the Front Line to get an idea of what the sector was like and see how the show went off. The front-line defences were still in their infancy compared with the Canadian trenches I'd visited a month before. A series of breast-high sentry-posts were connected by a shallow ditch, and no-man's-land was a cornfield which still seemed to be doing quite well. I was told that there was very little wire out in front. One felt that recent occupants of the sector had erred in the direction of a *laissez-faire* policy. It was a quiet moonless night, and the raiding-party, about a dozen strong, were assembled, and appeared to be doing their best to let the Germans know that they intended to come over. Stage whispers in broad Lancashire accents were making the best of an unhopeful situation, and I suspected that a double rum ration had been prematurely issued. (Rum rations should not precede raids.)

Why weren't they slipping across from some place where the trench was shallow, I wondered—instead of clambering clumsily over the parapet where it was highest? One by one they disappeared into the jungle of growing corn. The ensuing silence was accentuated by various sounds which clearly indicated human progress on all fours through a weak belt of barbed wire. Shortly afterwards the inevitable machine-gun demonstrated awareness of their whereabouts, flares went up from the other side, and there was a proper mix-up which ended when they blundered back, having achieved nothing but a few casualties less than half-way across. When the confusion had abated, I continued my instructive investigations for an hour or two, but the next thing that I clearly remember is that I was riding home in the early morning.

Quite distinctly I can recover a certain moment when I was trotting past the shuttered houses of some unawakened village, with the sun just coming up beyond the roadside poplars. What I felt was a sort of personal manifesto of being intensely alive—a sense of physical adventure and improvident jubilation; and also, as I looked at the signs of military occupation around me, a feeling that I was in the middle of some interesting historical tale. I was glad to be there, it seemed; and perhaps my thoughts for a moment revisited Slateford Hospital and were reminded of its unescapable atmosphere of humiliation. That was how active service used to hoodwink us. Wonderful moments in the War, we called them, and told people at home that after all we wouldn't have missed it for worlds. But it was only one's youngness, really, and the fact of being in a foreign country with a fresh mind. Not because of the War, but in spite of it, we felt such zest and fulfilment, and remembered it later on with nostalgic regret, forgetting the miseries and grumblings, and how we longed for it to come to an end. Nevertheless, there I was, a living antithesis to the gloomier entries in my diary, and a physical retraction of my last year's protest against the "political errors and insincerities for which the fighting men were being sacrificed".

But our inconsistencies are often what make us most interesting, and it is possible that, in my zeal to construct these memoirs carefully, I have eliminated too many of my own self-contradictions. Anyhow, human nature being what it is, I wasn't finding time to feel sorry for the raiding-party whose dud effort I'd recently witnessed. No; I was callously resolving to make a far better job of it with my own men, and wishing that I could consult the incomparable Captain Duclos. And I am afraid I was also cogitating about how I would demonstrate the superiority of A Company over the other three. My Company's officers were just up when I got back. I must have been tired out, for my only recollection of returning to St. Hilaire is of Velmore taking charge of my notebook and urging me to stop talking and swallow my breakfast before having a good sleep. Meanwhile he promised that he would faithfully expound to the Adjutant the details which I had accumulated.

*   *   *

That evening we relieved the East Lancashires. Nothing worth describing in that, I tell myself. But the remembering mind refuses to forget, and imbues the scene of past experience with significant finality. For when we marched away from the straggling village and out into the flat green fertile farmlands, the world did seem to be lit up as though for some momentous occasion. There had been thunder showers all the afternoon and the sunset flared with a sort of crude magnificence which dazzled us when our road took a sudden twist to the left. More memorable now, perhaps; but memorable even then, for me, whose senses were so teemingly alive as I gazed on that rich yet havoc-bordered landscape and thought of the darkness toward which we were going. The clouds flamed and the clover was crimson and the patches of tillage were vividly green as we splashed along between the poplars. And then, with dusk, the rain came down again as though to wash the picture out for ever.

We had five or six miles to go before we crossed the La Bassée Canal, and then it was another mile (with hundred yard intervals between platoons) to the rendezvous. Beyond the poplars was the ominous glare of the line, and the rattle of rifles and machine-guns competed with a local thunderstorm—"overhead artillery", one of the men called it. . . .

Here, at the cross roads, were the guides—quite a crowd of them, since we were the leading company. Two-minute intervals between platoons. Lead on Number One. I watched them file away into the gloom, while Velmore wiped his spectacles and conferred with the company sergeant-major in undertones. Lead on headquarters. And then a couple of miles easy walking brought us to the big shell-hole and its diminutive dug-outs. It was now one o'clock in the morning, and the relief was completed when I signed the list of trench-stores taken over. Referring to this document, I find that we "took over" 30,000 rounds of small arms ammunition, 12 gas gongs, 572 grenades, 120 shovels, 270 Véry lights, and 9 reaping hooks, besides other items too numerous to mention.

Howitt was the only platoon officer with the company. "Stiffy" had been made battalion Lewis-gun officer, and the other two were away on "courses". As I went up to

visit the trench-mortar battery on our left flank it struck
me that I was likely to have a fairly busy time while A
Company was being initiated into the mysteries of the
Western Front.

That didn't worry me, however, for I was, if anything, a
bit too much "on my toes", and the Great War had reduced itself to a little contest between my company and the
Central Powers, with Velmore standing by to send back
situation reports from our five hundred yard sector. Velmore, of course, was "on his toes" too, but in a more tem-
perate style than mine. His methods were unobtrusive but
thorough. While on this subject I must mention Sergeant
Wickham, who was more "on his toes" than any of us, and
had no alternative relaxations, such as ruminating or reading Flecker's poems. Wickham had been through the Boer
War, and had already won a D.C.M. and a Military
Medal in this one. But he wasn't resting on his laurels, and
having recently returned from a month's "refresher course"
at the army school, he was a complete embodiment of the
offensive spirit. I think he was one of the most delightful
N.C.O.s I've ever known. Except for being a little over-
excitable, he had all the qualities of a fine soldier including
the "women and children first" kind of chivalry, which
made it easy for one to imagine him as the last to leave the
sinking troopship. Always smart and cheerful—was Sergeant Wickham—and if ever a man deserved to be shaken
hands with by his Sovereign, it was he. During our first
twenty-four hours in the line, however, his adventurous
spirit discovered nothing sensational except a long-dead
German up in an old knotted willow; and in the evening
Velmore sent him down to the support-line with a working
party, though he was obviously aching to go out on patrol.

At about eleven o'clock I went out myself with Howitt
and a couple of N.C.O.s, but it was only in order to get
them accustomed to being out there. Everything was very
quiet while we crawled along the company front in the wet
corn. The Germans had sent over a few admonitory 5.9's
just after "stand-down"; at long intervals they fired their
machine-guns just to show they were still there. The topo-

graphy of our bit of no-man's-land was mainly agricultural, so our patrolling was easy work. On the right, B Company were demonstrating their offensive spirit by using up a fair amount of ammunition, but I had given orders that not a shot was to be fired by our Company. An impressively menacing silence prevailed, which, I hoped, would impress the Germans. I felt almost supercilious as I stood in the trench watching some B Company enthusiast experimenting with the Véry light pistol.

That was one of my untroubled moments, when I could believe that I'd got a firm grip on what I was doing and could be oblivious to the whys and wherefores of the war. I was standing beside Corporal Griffiths, who had his Lewis gun between his elbows on the dew-soaked parapet. His face, visible in the sinking light of a flare, had the look of a man who was doing his simple duty without demanding explanations from the stars above him. Vigilant and serious he stared straight ahead of him, and a fine picture of fortitude he made. He was only a stolid young farmer from Montgomeryshire; only; but such men, I think were England, in those dreadful years of war.

Thus the strangeness of the night wore on—and stranger still it seems while I am revisiting it from to-day—and after I'd been along to all the sentry-posts a second time, I went back to the headquarter rabbit-hole to find Velmore dozing, with Flecker's poems fallen from his hand, and the sturdy little sergeant-major dozing likewise in his own little rabbit-hole near by, while the signaller brooded over the buzzer. Away from the shell-hole there was another dug-out—larger, but not very deep—where we slept and had our food. Everything seems to be going on quite well, I thought, groping my way in, to sit there, tired and wakeful, and soaked and muddy from my patrol, while one candle made unsteady brown shadows in the gloom, and young Howitt lay dead beat and asleep in an ungainly attitude, with that queer half-sullen look on his face.

The thought of that candle haunts me now; I don't know why, except that it seems to symbolize the weary end of a night at the War, and that unforgettable remoteness from the ordinary existences which we might have been leading; Howitt going to an office in the morning; and Velmore down from that idyllic pre-war Oxford with an honours degree; and all those men in the company still unmobilized from farms and factories and wherever else it was they had earned a living.

I seem to be in that stuffy dug-out now, with Howitt snoring, and my wakeful watch ticking on the wrist which supported my head, and the deathly map of France and Flanders all around me in huge darkness receding to the distant boom of a big gun. I seem to be back in my mind as it then was—a mind whose haggard vigilance had the power to deny its body rest, while with the clairvoyance of sleeplessness it strove to be detached from clogging discomfort and to achieve, in its individual isolation, some sort of mastery over the experience which it shared with those dead and sleeping multitudes, of whom young Howitt was the visible representation.

I wanted to know—to understand—before it was too late, whether there was any meaning in this human tragedy which sprawled across France, while those who planned yet further slaughter were like puppets directing operations on which the unknown gods had turned their backs in boredom with our blundering bombardments. I wanted to know the reason why Corporal Griffiths was being what he was in quiet fortitude.

And I felt a great longing to be liberated from these few hundred yards of ant-like activity—to travel all the way along the Western Front—to learn through my eyes and with my heart the organism of this monstrous drama which my mind had not the power to envision as a whole. But my mind could see no further than the walls of that dug-out with its one wobbling candle which now burnt low. Universalization of military experience fizzled out in my thinking that some day we should look back on these St. Floris trenches as a sort of Paradise compared with places in which we had afterwards found ourselves. Unlike those ditches and earthworks which had become fetid with recurrent human catastrophes—hummocks and slag-heaps and

morasses whose names would live for ever in war histories
—ours was an almost innocent sector, still recognizable as
cultivated farmland. I could recognize that innocence
when Bond had made me some tea, and I had emerged
into the peace of daybreak. The pollard willows loomed
somewhat strange and ominous against the sky, but before
long I was looking out over the parapet at an immaculate
morning, with St. Floris away on the left—a factory chim-
ney rising from a huddle of mysterious roofs—mysterious
only because they were on the edge of no-man's-land.

Aloof from our concerns, another day was beginning,
and there seemed no special reason why the War should
command us to keep our heads down. The country, as I
said before, looked innocent; the morning air was like life's
elixir, and hope went singing skyward with the lark.

*   *   *

Refreshed by a few hours' sleep, I was up in the Front
Line an hour or two after midday, gazing at the incalculable country beyond the cornfield. My map told me that
the town of Merville was about three miles away from me,
but the level landscape prevented it from being visible.
Our long-range gunners knew a lot about Merville, no
doubt, but it was beyond my horizon, and I couldn't hear
so much as a rumble of wheels coming from that direction.
The outlook was sunlit and completely silent, for it was the
quietest time of day.

I was half-way between two sentry-posts, on the extreme
left of our sector, where no-man's-land was narrowest. The
longer I stared at the cornfield the more I wanted to know
what was on the other side, and this inquisitiveness gradually developed into a determination. Discarding all my
obligations as Company Commander (my main obligation
being to remain inside the trench and get it deepened by
those 120 shovels, which we'd taken over) I took off all my
equipment, strolled along to the nearest sentry, borrowed
his bayonet, and told him that I was going out to have a
look at the wire. Returning to my equipment, I added my
tunic and steel helmet to the heap, took a deep breath,

grasped the bayonet firmly in my right hand, and crawled out into the unknown. I wasn't doing this from a sense of duty. It would certainly be helpful if I could find out exactly what things were like on the other side, and whether, as was rumoured by staff experts, the Germans withdrew most of their trench garrison during the day. But my uppermost idea was, I must admit, that the first man of the 74th Division to arrive in the enemy trenches was going to be me. This was a silly idea and I deserved no credit at all for it. Relying on Velmore to hold the fort at company headquarters, I was lapsing into my rather feckless 1916 self. It was, in fact, what I called "playing my natural game". I can't believe that I really enjoyed it, but it was exciting to worm one's way across, trying not to rustle the corn stalks. After about 300 yards of this sort of thing I crept through a few strands of wire and came to the edge of the concealment zone. What on earth would Doctor Macamble say if he could see me, I wondered, trying to bluff myself into a belief that I wasn't the least bit nervous. He would probably have rebuked me for being "bloodthirsty"; but I didn't feel at all like that.

The shallow German trench was only a few yards away, and there was no one in it, which was a great relief to my mind. I got into it as quickly as I could and then sat down, feeling by no means at home. The bayonet in my hand didn't seem to give me any extra confidence, but there were some stick-bombs lying about, so I picked one up, thinking that it would be just as well to take something back as a surprise for old Velmore. I then proceeded along the trench, sedately but bent double. For the benefit of those who enjoy exact description I will add that I was going in the direction of the Germans who were opposite B Company, i.e. away from St. Floris. The trench was only waist-deep; almost at once I saw what I presumed to be a machine-gun team. There were four of them, and they were standing about thirty yards away, gazing in the other direction. They were wearing flat blue-grey caps and their demeanour suggested boredom and idleness. Anyhow I was at last more or less in contact with the enemies of

England. I had come from Edinburgh via Limerick and Jerusalem, drawing full pay for seven months, and I could now say that I had seen some of the people I was fighting against. And what I saw was four harmless young Germans who were staring up at a distant aeroplane.

Standing upright, I watched them with breathless interest until one of them turned and looked me straight in the face. He was a blond youth of Saxon type, and he registered complete astonishment. For several seconds we gaped at one another; then he turned to draw the attention of his companions to their unknown visitor, who immediately betook himself to the cover of the cornfield, to the best of his ability imitating a streak of light. I returned much quicker than I came, and while the Germans were talking it over at their leisure I resumed my tunic and tin hat and took the bayonet back to its owner who eyed the stick-bomb enquiringly. With a marked change of manner from my recent retreat on all fours, I laconically mentioned that I'd just slipped across and fetched it. I then returned in triumph to Velmore, who implored me not to do that sort of thing again without warning him.

We thereupon decided that, as the general had announced that he expected a prisoner as soon as possible, the obvious thing to do was to send Howitt across with a strong patrol some fine morning to bring back that machine-gun team and thus acquire a Military Cross. It had been great fun, I felt. And I regarded myself as having scored a point against the people who had asserted that I was suffering from shell-shock.

* * *

About ten o'clock that night I hunched my way into the rabbit-hole feeling somewhat the worse for wear. "Slight strafe on, it seems!" I remarked to Velmore, who was leaning his back against the far end where there was just room for the pair of us to sit side by side.

"We must try and stop the men moving about so much round headquarters by day," he suggested. I lit my pipe. There was no doubt they'd fairly put the wind up me a few

minutes before when a batch of 5.9's had dropped all
round me while I lay flat on the ground somewhere between number 8 and 9 sentry-posts. Velmore sympathized
and commented on the accuracy of the Teutonic artillery-
men. The Adjutant had been up that evening and had told
him that a big shell had landed just outside Orderly Room
window about breakfast time. Luckily it had fallen on the
manure-heap. A thud and an earth-shaking explosion immediately behind our dug-out now caused me to propose
that a spot of Flecker wouldn't do us any harm, and we had
just begun to make the Golden Journey to Samarkand
when another shell arrived plump on top of us. But there
was no explosion. The smoke still curled up from Velmore's cigarette. "Our camels sniff the evening and are
glad," quoted he. . . . A large fissure had appeared in the
earth wall behind us; exactly between us the nose-cap of
the shell protruded. Velmore, who had a talent for pictur-
esque phrases, named the crack in the wall "the grin of
death". I still consider it queer that only the dudness of
that 5.9 preserved us from becoming the débris of a direct
hit.

Consulting my watch, I found that it was time for me to
be taking out my conducted tours in no-man's-land. (I
took them out, two at a time, for twenty-minute crawls,
and the "patrol proper" went out at 12.30.) "I think I'll
come up with you," remarked Velmore. "It can't be more
dangerous in the Front Line than it is here."

*   *   *

On the following night at much the same time we were
squatting in exactly the same place, munching chocolate.
We were agreeing that the company was getting through
its first dose of the line extremely well. They were a fine
steady lot, and had worked hard at strengthening the posts
and deepening the shallow connecting trench. We had also
improved the wire. Best of all, we should be relieved the
next night. "And not a single casualty so far," said Velmore. I didn't touch wood, but as to-morrow was the thir-
teenth I produced my fire-opal and touched that. "Aren't

opals supposed to be unlucky?" he enquired dubiously, shutting one eye while he admired the everlasting sunset glories of the jewel. "Mine isn't," I replied, adding that I intended to give it another test that night. "I'm going to do a really good patrol," I announced. Velmore looked worried and said he wished I wouldn't. He argued that there was no special reason for doing it. I reminded him that we must maintain our supremacy in no-man's-land. "Haven't you already shown your damned supremacy by going over and quelling the Fritzes with a look?" he protested. But I produced a plausible project. I was going to locate a machine-gun which had seemed to be firing from outside their trench with the intention of enfilading us, and anyhow it was all arranged, and I was going out with Corporal Davies at one o'clock, from No. 14 post (which was where our company front ended). Seeing that I was bent on going, Velmore became helpful, and the sergeant-major was told to send an urgent warning to B Company, as the objective I had in mind was on their front.

My real reason for seeking trouble like this was my need to escape from the worry and responsibility of being a Company Commander, plus annoyance with the idea of being blown to bits while sitting there watching Velmore inditing a nicely-worded situation report. I was tired and over-strained, and my old foolhardiness was taking control of me.

To be outside the trench with the possibility of bumping into an enemy patrol was at any rate an antidote to my suppressed weariness of the entire bloody business. I wanted to do something definite, and perhaps get free of the whole thing. It was the old story; I could only keep going by doing something spectacular.

So there was more bravado than bravery about it, and I should admire that vanished self of mine more if he had avoided taking needless risks. I blame him for doing his utmost to prevent my being here to write about him. But on the other hand I am grateful to him for giving me something to write about.

*   *   *

Leaving me in the rabbit-hole to ruminate and reserve my energies, Velmore toddled off to the Front Line, which was, to revert to golfing phraseology, only an easy iron-shot away. I cannot claim that I remember exactly what I ruminated about, but an intimate knowledge of my mental technique assures me that, with danger looming in the near future, my thoughts were soon far away from St. Floris. (Who was St. Floris, by the way?) Probably I scribbled half a page in that long lost notebook—not too self-consciously, I hope. And then my mind may have rambled off to see a few friends.

Having ceased to wonder when the War would be over, I couldn't imagine myself anywhere else but on active service, and I was no longer able to indulge in reveries about being at home. When I came out this last time I had turned my back on everything connected with peace-time enjoyment. I suppose this meant that I was making a forced effort to keep going till the end. Like many people, I had a feeling that ordinary human existence was being converted into a sort of nightmare. Things were being said and done which would have been considered madness before the War. The effects of the War had been the reverse of ennobling, it seemed. Social historians can decide whether I am wrong about it.

Anyhow, as I was saying, I probably thought vaguely about those kind hunting people at Limerick, and speculated on such problems as what The Mister did with himself during the summer months; it quite worried me when I thought of the old boy convivially consuming neat whisky in hot weather. But if I called to mind my more intimate friends, it was themselves that I saw and not the places where I had been happy with them.

And if my visual meditations included the face of Rivers I did not allow myself to consult him as to the advisability of avoiding needless risks. I knew that he would have dissuaded me from doing that patrol. And then, no doubt, I dozed off until Velmore came back to tell me that it was getting on for one o'clock and Corporal Davies all ready for me up at No. 14 post.

Corporal Davies was a trained scout, young, small and active. We had worked out our little scheme, such as it was, and he now informed me in a cheerful whisper that the machine-gun which was our objective had been firing now and again from its usual position, which was half-right, about four hundred yards away. (The German trench was about six hundred yards from ours at that point.) In my pocket I had my little automatic pistol to provide moral support, and we took three or four Mills' bombs apiece. Our intention was to get as near as we could and then put the wind up the machine-gunners with our bombs.

A sunken farm-road ran out from No. 14 post; along this we proceeded with intense caution. About a hundred yards out we forsook the road and bore right-handed. It was a warm still night and the moon was very properly elsewhere, but the clear summer sky diminished the darkness and one could see quite a lot after a bit. Under such conditions every clod of earth was liable to look like the head of a recumbent enemy and the rustle of a fieldmouse in the corn could cause a certain trepidation—intrepid trepidation, of course.

Obviously it takes a longish time to crawl three or four hundred yards with infinite caution, but as nothing occurred to hinder our progress there is nothing narratable about it. I hadn't the time on me; crawling on my stomach might have smashed my watch-glass if it had been in my pocket, and its luminosity would have been out of place on my wrist. But what a relief it was, to be away from time and its petty tyrannies, even when one's heart was in one's mouth.

Behind us loomed the sentry-posts and the impressive sweep of the line, where poor old Velmore was peering anxiously out while he awaited our return. It really felt as though Corporal Davies and I had got the best of it out there. We were beyond all interference by Brigadiers.

Just when I least expected it the German machine-gun fired a few rounds, for no apparent reason except to allow us to locate it. We were, as far as I could judge, less than fifty yards from it and it seemed uncomfortably near. I looked at Davies, whose countenance was only too visible, for the sky was growing pale and we must have been out there well over two hours. Davies needed no prompting. He had already pulled out the pin of a bomb. So, to cut a long story short, we crawled a bit nearer, loosed off the lot, and retreated with the rapidity of a pair of scared badgers. I don't for a moment suppose that we hit anybody, but the deed was done, and when we were more than half-way home I dropped into the sunken road, and only the fact that I was out on a patrol prevented me from slapping my leg with a loud guffaw.

*   *   *

Now that it was all over I was exuberantly excited. It had been tremendous fun, and that was all there was to say about it. Davies agreed, and his fresh young face seemed to be asserting not only our supremacy over no-man's-land, but the supreme satisfaction of being alive on a perfect summer's morning after what might be called a strenuous military escapade. Taking off my tin hat I allowed my head to feel glad to be relieved of the weight of the War, and there, for several minutes, we sat leaning against the bank and recovering our breath.

It seemed hardly worth while to continue our return journey on all fours, as we were well hidden from the German trenches; the embankment of No. 14 Post was just visible above the corn stalks and my conscience reminded me that Velmore's anxiety ought to be put an end to at once. With my tin hat in my hand I stood up and turned for a moment to look back at the German line.

A second later I was down again, half stunned by a terrific blow on the head. It seemed to me that there was a very large hole in the right side of my skull. I felt, and believed, that I was as good as dead. Had this been so I should have been unconscious of anything, but that idea didn't strike me.

Ideas were a thing of the past now. While the blood poured from my head, I was intensely aware of everything around me—the clear sky and the ripening corn and the early glow of sunrise on the horrified face of the little red-haired corporal who knelt beside me. I saw it all as though for the last time, and my whole body and being were possessed by a dreadful sense of unhappiness. Body and spirit were one, and both must perish. The world had been mine, and the fullness of life, and in a moment all had been changed and I was to lose it.

I had been young and exuberant, and now I was just a dying animal, on the verge of oblivion.

And then a queer thing happened. My sense of humour stirred in me, and—emerging from that limbo of desolate defeat—I thought "I suppose I ought to say something special—last words of dying soldier".... And do you know that I take great pride in that thought because I consider that it showed a certain invincibility of mind; for I really did believe that I was booked for the Roll of Honour. I need hardly say that I wasn't; after a bit the corporal investigated my head and became optimistic, and I plucked up courage and dared to wonder whether, perhaps, I was in such a bad way after all. And the end of it was that I felt very much better and got myself back to No. 14 Post without any assistance from Davies, who carried my tin hat for me.

Velmore's face was a study in mingled concern and relief, but the face of Sergeant Wickham was catastrophic.

For Wickham was there, and it was he who had shot me.

The fact was that his offensive spirit had led him astray. He had heard the banging of our bombs and had been so much on his toes that he'd forgotten to go and find out whether we had returned. Over-eager to accomplish something spectacular, he had waited and watched; and when he spotted someone approaching our trench had decided that the Germans were about to raid us. I was told afterwards that when he'd fired at me he rushed out shouting, "Surrender—you ——!" Which only shows what a gallant man he was—though everyone knew that already. It also showed that although he'd heard me lecturing to the company N.C.O.s on my "Four C's—i.e.—Confidence, Co-operation, Common sense, and Consolidation"—he had

that morning been co-operating with nothing except his
confident ambition to add a bar to his D.C.M. (which,
I am glad to say, he ultimately did).

I suppose it was partly my fault. Both of us ought to have
known better than to behave like that. The outcome was
absurd, but logical. And to say that I was well out of it is an
understatement of an extremely solemn fact.

III

Thus ended my last week at the War. And there, perhaps,
my narrative also should end. For I seem to write these
words of someone who never returned from France, someone whose effort to succeed in that final experience was
finished when he lay down in the sunken road and wondered
what he ought to say.

I state this quite seriously, though I am aware that it
sounds somewhat nonsensical. But even now I wonder how
it was that Wickham's bullet didn't go through my skull
instead of only furrowing my scalp. For it had been a fixed
idea of mine that something like that would happen.
Amateur psychologists will say that I had a "death-wish",
I suppose. But that seems to me to be much the same as
wanting peace at any price, so we won't argue about it.

Anyhow I see a sort of intermediate version of myself,
who afterwards developed into what I am now; I see him
talking volubly to Velmore and Howitt on the way back to
company H.Q.; and saying good-bye with a bandaged
head and assuring them that he'd be back in a week or two,
and then walking down to battalion H.Q., with his faithful
batman Bond carrying his haversack and equipment; and
then talking rather wildly to the Adjutant and Major
Evans (who was now in command), and finally getting
into the motor ambulance which took him to the casualty
clearing station.

And two days later he is still talking rather wildly, but
he is talking to himself now, and scribbling it down with a
pencil as he lies in a bed at No. 8 Red Cross Hospital,

Boulogne. It is evidence of what I have just written, so I will reproduce it.

"I don't know how to begin this. It is meant to be a confession of my real feelings, or an attempt to find out what they really are. Time drifts between me and last week. Everything gets blurred. I know that I feel amputated from the battalion. It seemed all wrong to be leaving the Company behind and going away into safety. I told the company sergeant-major I should be back soon and then climbed out of the headquarters shell-hole. Down the path between wheat and oats and beans, and over the dangerous willow-bordered road until I came to the red-roofed farm. Five o'clock on a July morning. . . . I passed the little cluster of crosses, and blundered into the Aid Post to get my head seen to. Prolonged farewells to the C.O. and other H.Q. officers—sleepy men getting situation reports from the Front Line. 'You'll see me back in three weeks' I shouted, and turned the corner of the lane with a last confident gesture. And so from one dressing station to another, to spend a night at the big C.C.S. where I tried to persuade an R.A.M.C. Colonel to keep me there till my head was healed. Even now I hang on to my obsession about not going to Blighty. I write to people at home saying that I'm staying in France till I can go up to the line again. And I do it with an angry tortured feeling. 'I'll stay here just to spite those blighters who yell about our infamous enemies,' is what I think, and then I wonder what the hell I am to them. If I'd moved my head an inch I'd be dead now, and what would the patriots care? . . . Then I remember the kindly face of my servant, and see him putting my kit on to the ambulance. I smile at him and say 'Back soon,' and he promises to walk over to the C.C.S. next day with my letters and the latest news from the company. But I'd gone when he got there. . . . They'd sent me on to a place near St. Omer. If I'd kicked up a row and refused to go they'd have thought I was dotty, especially with a head wound. Who ever heard of anyone refusing to go down to the Base with a decent wound? Now I'm at Boulogne trying to be hearty and well. It's only a scalp-graze, I say; but I dare

not look the doctor in the face. It isn't all of me that wants
to stay in France now.

"Nurses make a fuss over me till I scarcely dare to behave like a healthy man.

"And still the memory of the Company haunts me and
wrings my heart and I hear them saying 'When's the Captain coming back?' It seems as if there's nothing to go back
to in England as long as the War goes on. Up in the line I
was at least doing something real, and I had lived myself
into a feeling of responsibility—inefficient and impulsive
though I was when in close contact with the Germans. All
that was decent in me disliked leaving Velmore and Howitt
and the troops. But now I begin to tell myself that perhaps
half of them will be casualties by the time I get back, and I
ask how many officers there are in the battalion who would
refuse to go to England if it were made easy for them.

"Not one, I believe; so why should I be the only one.
They'd only think me a fool, if they knew I'd gone back on
purpose to be with them.

"Yet it is the supreme thing that is asked of me, and
already I am shying at it. 'We'll be sending you across to
England in a few days,' murmurs the nurse while she is
dabbing my head. She says it quite naturally, as if it were
the only possible thing that could happen. I close my eyes,
and all I can see is the door into the garden at home and
Aunt Evelyn coming in with her basket of flowers. In a
final effort to quell those cravings for safety I try to see in
the dark the far-off vision of the line, with flares going up
and the whine and crash of shells scattered along the level
dusk. Men flitting across the gloom; low voices challenging
—'Halt; who are you?' Someone gasping by, carrying a
bag of rations—'Jesus, ain't we there yet?'—then he blunders into a shell-hole and crouches there while bullets hiss
overhead. I see the sentries in the forward posts, staring
patiently into the night—sombre shapes against a flickering sky. Oh yes, I see it all, from A to Z! Then I listen to
the chatter of the other wounded officers in this room,
talking about people being blown to bits. And I remember
a man at the C.C.S. with his jaw blown off by a bomb—

('a fine-looking chap, he was,' they said). He lay there with one hand groping at the bandages which covered his whole head and face, gurgling every time he breathed. His tongue was tied forward to prevent him swallowing it. The War had gagged him—smashed him—and other people looked at him and tried to forget what they'd seen. . . . All this I remember, while the desirable things of life, like living phantoms, steal quietly into my brain, look wistfully at me, and steal away again—beckoning, pointing—'to England in a few days'. . . . And though it's wrong I know I shall go there, because it is made so easy for me."

IV

On February 13th I had landed in France and again become part of the war machine which needed so much flesh and blood to keep it working. On July 20th the machine automatically returned me to London, and I was most carefully carried into a perfect hospital.

There, in a large ward whose windows overlooked Hyde Park, I lay and listened to the civilian rumour of London traffic which seemed to be specially subdued for the benefit of the patients. In this apotheosis (or nirvana) of physical comfort, I had no possible cause for complaint, and my only material adversity was the fact that while at Boulogne I had hung my opal talisman on the bedpost and someone had succumbed to the temptation. But the opal, as I reminded myself, had done its work, and I tried to regard its disappearance as symbolical. Sunday passed peacefully, graciously signalized by a visit from two members of the Royal Family, who did their duty with the maximum amount of niceness and genuine feeling. For the best part of a minute I was an object of sympathetic interest, and I really felt that having succeeded in becoming a casualty, I was doing the thing in the best possible style.

On the Monday I became comparatively active and instructed one of my friends to order a gramophone to be sent to A Company, plus a few "comforts" for the officers.

But Velmore and the others had vanished; their remoteness became more apparent every day, though I rejoiced when I received Velmore's letter announcing that Howitt had been across no-man's-land with ten men and had brought back five Germans and a machine-gun—these being the first prisoners captured by the 74th Division in France.

Outwardly I was being suavely compensated for whatever exactions the war machine had inflicted on me. I had nothing to do except lie there and wonder whether it was possible to be more comfortable, even though I'd got a half-healed hole in my head. But inwardly I was restless and overwrought. My war had stopped, but its after-effects were still with me. I couldn't sleep, so after a few days I was moved into a room where there was only one other bed, which was unoccupied. But in there my brain became busier than ever; the white-walled room seemed to imprison me, and my thoughts couldn't escape from themselves into that completed peace which was the only thing I wanted. I saw myself as one who had achieved nothing except an idiotic anti-climax, and my mind worked itself into a tantrum of self-disparagement. Why hadn't I stayed in France where I could at least escape from the War by being in it? Out there I had never despised my existence as I did now.

Life had seemed a glorious and desirable thing in those moments when I was believing that the bullet had finished me off, when it had seemed as if the living soul in me also was about to be extinguished. And now that angry feeling of wanting to be killed came over me—as though I were looking at my living self and longing to bash its silly face in. My little inferno was then interrupted by a nurse who brought me my tea. What the hell was wrong with me? I wondered, becoming less irrational and exasperated. And I told myself that if I wasn't careful I should go from bad to worse, realizing that the sun had been shining in at the window all the afternoon and I'd been lying there tearing myself to pieces and feeling miserable and frustrated. I suppose my nerves really are a bit rotten, I thought, lighting my pipe and trying to be sensible. But I was still worried by feeling so inglorious. I was nearly thirty-two and nothing that I'd done seemed to have been any good. There was some consolation in the feeling that one wasn't as old as one's age, but when I tried to think about the future I found that I couldn't see it. There was no future except "the rest of the War", and I didn't want that. My knight-errantry about the War had fizzled out in more ways than one, and I couldn't go back to being the same as I was before it started. The "good old days" had been pleasant enough in their way, but what could a repetition of them possibly lead to?

How could I begin my life all over again when I had no conviction about anything except that the War was a dirty trick which had been played on me and my generation? That, at any rate, was something to be angry and bitter about now that everything had fallen to pieces and one's mind was in a muddle and one's nerves were all on edge. . . .

Yes; my mind was in a muddle; and it seemed that I had learned but one thing from being a soldier—that if we continue to accept war as a social institution we must also recognize that the Prussian system is the best, and Prussian militarism must be taught to children in schools. They must be taught to offer their finest instincts for exploitation by the unpitying machinery of scientific warfare. And they must not be allowed to ask why they are doing it.

And then, unexpected and unannounced, Rivers came in and closed the door behind him. Quiet and alert, purposeful and unhesitating, he seemed to empty the room of everything that had needed exorcising.

My futile demons fled him—for his presence was a refutation of wrong-headedness. I knew then that I had been very lonely while I was at the War; I knew that I had a lot to learn, and that he was the only man who could help me.

Without a word he sat down by the bed; and his smile was benediction enough for all I'd been through. "Oh, Rivers, I've had such a funny time since I saw you last!" I exclaimed. And I understood that this was what I'd been waiting for.

He did not tell me that I had done my best to justify his belief in me. He merely made me feel that he took all that for granted, and now we must go on to something better still. And this was the beginning of the new life toward which he had shown me the way. . . .

It has been a long journey from that moment to this, when I write the last words of my book. And my last words shall be these—that it is only from the inmost silences of the heart that we know the world for what it is, and ourselves for what the world has made us.